MISADVENTURES ON THE NIGHT SHIFT

BY
LAUREN ROWE

MISADVENTURES
ON THE
NIGHT SHIFT

BY
LAUREN ROWE

WATERHOUSE PRESS

This book is dedicated to those of us with blue skin.
May we always find the courage not to hide it.

CHAPTER ONE

"Holy shit," Danica whispers, staring at something on her phone at the other end of the check-in counter. "Abby, you've got to see this."

I don't look up from my textbook, as usual. No offense to my darling Danica Reynolds and her never-ending search for porny distractions at work, but I don't have time to gawk at man meat right now, especially not when we've finally reached The Dead Zone portion of our shift, the much-appreciated two- to three-hour window when nothing ever happens and I can finally study without interruption.

"Abby," Danica persists. "You've got to see this."

"Babe, I've got to get through this reading assignment before starting on the checkout folios."

"Bah, studying can wait. I'm looking at Lucas Ford over here."

My head jerks up from my textbook like a golden retriever whose owner just threw a stick. If there's one man on the planet who could lure me away from studying about wrongful termination under the Civil Rights Act of 1964, it's the sexiest rock star on the planet. The man whose face decorated my teenage walls ten years ago. Lucas Ford.

But, no, I really shouldn't take a peek.

I look back down at my book.

Being able to get some solid studying done at work was the sole reason I agreed to be assigned to the God-awful night shift at this hotel in the first place, and I can't afford to waste optimal study time gawking at men, even if the man in question happens to be my teenage fantasy. Okay, yeah, my fifteen-year-old self is punching me in the proverbial balls right now for not taking a peek at the photo on Danica's phone, but the stressed-out twenty-four-year-old I've become has bigger fish to fry than giving my inner teenager a lady-boner. "I've got to study," I mutter, continuing to look down at my textbook.

"You're such a prude." Danica chastises me, but her tone is affectionate. "Live a little for once, Abby. Take a walk on the wild side."

I smirk to myself. Oh, Danica. I love her and I know she loves me. But she only knows the version of me who's worked here for the past two years. If she'd known me five years ago when I was a human grenade, she'd never in a million years dream of telling me to walk on the wild side.

"Lucas Ford is playing tomorrow night at the arena," Danica says, still staring at her phone. "The show's sold out but I bet you could score tickets online. He's one of your favorites, right?"

"Yeah. I'd love to go, but I'm working tomorrow night. Aren't you off tomorrow night? You should go."

"No, I picked up an extra shift from Tammy. I'm still trying to save up to help my mom." She sighs. "I'm bummed. I've never seen Lucas Ford in concert. It's definitely on my bucket list."

"Oh, he's phenomenal. I saw him nine or ten years ago, right when 'Shattered Hearts' first came out, and he absolutely slayed it. The minute he started playing the opening guitar riff, I burst into tears, even before he started singing."

"Ha! I would have done exactly the same thing back then. Actually, I'd probably burst into tears today. That's still my all-time favorite song."

"Mine, too."

She snickers. "I lost my virginity to it."

"Really? Did you choose the song or did the guy?"

"The guy, but only because he knew I loved it. It would have been a fantastic memory for me if only he'd lasted past the first chorus."

We both guffaw at that.

Of course, if I were a normal girl who chatted breezily with her girlfriends about sex, now would probably be the perfect moment to tell Danica about how I gave myself my first orgasm at the tender age of fifteen while listening to "Shattered Hearts" and staring longingly at its creator's twenty-year-old face on my bedroom wall. But, of course, since I'm not a normal girl, I've set certain non-negotiable rules for myself to keep my life on track. And one of those is never to talk about sex at work. Not even with Danica. Which means I keep my mouth firmly shut.

I look down at my textbook again and try to concentrate, but Danica's loud snickering as she stares at her phone is awfully hard to ignore. I look at her again and sigh. "Are you still looking at that same photo of Lucas Ford or have you moved on to Jamie Dornan or Charlie Hunnam now?"

"I'm still looking at Lucas Ford. And it's not his photo. It's a *video*." She smiles broadly. "A sex tape, actually."

My eyebrows shoot up.

"It got leaked tonight," Danica continues, barely containing a giggle. "And lemme just say, all those rumors about Lucas Ford having an extremely large package? They're all true."

I feel color rise in my cheeks. I look around to confirm nobody's entering the empty lobby at this particular moment. "You can see his dick in the video?" I whisper.

"Every inch. At the beginning of the sex tape, Lucas walks right in front of the camera, completely naked, like he's a peacock showing off, and you can see *everything*—dick, balls, tattoos, his eight-pack. The whole nine yards. And then, two seconds later, he starts screwing his girlfriend from behind and you can totally see his hard-on sliding in and out of her and his balls swinging. Good stuff."

My cheeks are flooding with heat. And so is my crotch.

Danica smiles slyly. "Come see the show, Abby...if you dare."

I shouldn't do it. How many times did Dr. Carlson warn me off watching porn back in the day? "It's a trigger for you, Abby," she always used to say. "And you need to avoid triggers at all costs."

"Holy hell," Danica says. "That's a beautiful dick."

I bite my lip. Maybe I should make an exception to my rules, just this once. I haven't had a problem in years and I'm a grown-ass woman now, not a teenager with zero impulse control. Surely, one little peek at my favorite rock star bonin' his girlfriend in a video isn't going to send me spiraling into the hinterlands of hell.

I close my textbook and lurch down the short length of the check-in counter until I'm literally draped over Danica's shoulder, looking at her phone. "Start it from the beginning, baby."

Danica squeals, obviously enthralled at my uncharacteristic

willingness to partake in her favorite pastime, and she quickly restarts the video.

And...I'm...instantly enthralled by what I see.

"Holy moly," I whisper. "That's quite a dick."

Danica giggles. "Told ya."

"He's absolutely beautiful."

Mr. Rock Star is standing before the camera, naked and fully erect, every square inch of him on glorious display from head to toe, while a buxom blonde bends over what looks like a hotel bed behind him, her thighs spread, her fingers unmistakably working herself between her legs.

After pumping on his hard dick a few times, Lucas strides to the blonde, his muscles taut, and takes over the job of fingering her.

A half-minute later, the woman cries out from apparent pleasure, which prompts Lucas to fist her blond hair, slide that massive dick of his inside her, and begin screwing her to within an inch of her life.

"Whoa," I whisper.

"No smoke and mirrors here, folks," Danica whispers back. "This is definitely not a simulation."

I clutch my chest. My heart's beating so hard, I feel like I'm going to pass out. "He's..." But I don't finish my sentence. Gorgeous? Spectacular? A fantasy come to life? Any of these descriptors would be accurate, but none of them would do him justice.

"He's a beast," Danica says, finishing my sentence for me. "Look how hard he's pulling on her hair. Good lord."

"I don't think she minds," I whisper back, my heart and clit pounding in equal measure.

"Lucky bitch," Danica whispers. "I'd pay my life savings to have that man fuck me like that."

"Your life savings amounts to about three dollars and eighty-seven cents," I whisper, my eyes still trained on the video.

"Yeah, and Lucas Ford can have it all!"

We both giggle.

"Jesus, he's fucking the living hell out of her, isn't he?" Danica says. "Lucky, lucky bitch."

"Yeah, she definitely seems..." I say, but I trail off again mid-sentence, too distracted by what's happening onscreen. Namely, while still screwing the blonde, Lucas Ford has just turned his head and is looking straight at the camera...*and he's not looking away*.

Hot damn, he's giving me goose bumps with that unwavering stare of his. Of course, intellectually, I know Lucas and the blonde are alone in that hotel room and he's staring at nothing but a mounted camera, but it sure *feels* like he's staring right at his audience, getting off on the idea of people watching him. And, honestly, that's a massive turn-on to me.

"Happy," Danica says.

"Huh?" I reply, my clit throbbing.

"She definitely seems *happy*," Danica says, finishing my last sentence.

"Oh. Yeah." I clear my throat. "She sure does."

"She's a real bitch for leaking the video." Danica sniffs. "I heard she got paid a million bucks by some tabloid. *Bitch*."

I mumble something incoherent, too entranced to speak. Surely, this precise image is the one I'll call to mind every time I touch myself for the rest of my life. Lucas Ford's piercing dark eyes staring into mine as his massive glistening cock slides in and out of another woman's pussy, his fist buried in her hair, his beautiful muscles tensing and releasing with each beastly thrust.

"He's so hot," Danica breathes.

I nod my agreement but remain mute. Lucas is about to come in the video—*I can feel it*—and I don't want to be chatting casually with Danica when he does. No, when Lucas experiences euphoria, I want to be able to give him my undivided attention. Because as turned on as I'm feeling right now, I'm going to come right along with him.

"Oh, fuck," Lucas suddenly blurts in the video. He pulls out of the blonde, spins her around, and pushes her roughly onto the bed, a maneuver that makes her very large breasts jiggle wildly.

I lean into the screen, holding my breath, my lower abdomen tight and aching for release, and watch as Lucas grabs his massive, straining cock like a fire hose, glowers over the woman's torso, and—

The video abruptly ends.

"No!" Danica stage-whispers, taking the word right out of my mouth. She taps on her screen violently, obviously thinking there's been some kind of glitch. But, nope, the video's over. "Damn it!" Danica says. "We don't get to see Lucas Ford's happy ending? Talk about lady-blue-balls." She laughs.

But I can't laugh with Danica. Hell no. An aching, throbbing, unrelieved clit isn't what I'd call a comedic situation. "Excuse me," I say curtly, striding around the front desk and beelining toward the restrooms on the far side of the lobby.

"Aw, why you always got to be such a prude, Abigail Medford?" she calls after me playfully as I stride away. "You can't watch a sex tape *once* in your life without feeling guilty about it?" She laughs.

"Poor, poor Abby. Always thinks she's going to hell."

Without replying to Danica, I enter the restrooms, head straight into a stall, pull down my panties, and finger my aching, swollen clit until I come. And I do, *hard*, in all of about twelve seconds flat.

CHAPTER TWO

"Yes, sir," Danica says next to me at the check-in counter, talking on the phone with one of the guests. "I understand, sir. We'll handle it." She hangs up and rolls her eyes. "Another noise complaint from Mr. Anthony in seven oh one."

"Sucks to be you," I say, not looking up from the folios I'm preparing for the morning's checkouts.

"I'll finish up the folios if you handle the noise complaint this time," Danica says. "I chased down all the noise complaints last night."

"Oh, no you didn't, you liar. I handled three right before we watched the Lucas Ford porno, remember?"

"Oh, yeah. That's right. Shoot."

"Your turn tonight, babycakes. Have fun."

"Okay, okay." Danica begins moving around the front desk. "Speaking of the rock star with the gigantic cock, did you hear? It's all over the internet. Lucas Ford had some sort of meltdown at his concert tonight. He flipped off the audience and marched offstage, mid-set, even before playing 'Shattered Hearts.' Apparently, he left his band standing there, like, 'Wha...?' I feel sorry for anyone who bought a ticket."

"No, I didn't see that. And you know why? Because, unlike you,

I've been working all night. Off you go, babe. Say hi to Mr. Seven Oh One for me."

Danica waves dismissively. "Yeah, yeah." She strides across the lobby toward the elevator bank, flipping her dark hair and swinging her hips as she goes.

I look down at my work again, but before I can get too far into it, the outside line rings. "The Rockford Hotel," I say, pressing the phone into my ear. "How may I help you?"

"Do you have a penthouse suite available tonight?" a nerdy male voice asks. "I need it for about a week. It's for a high-profile individual."

I'm not surprised by the high-profile individual thing. We get that a lot at The Rockford, even at this Denver location, although surely our Los Angeles and New York sister locations attract celebrity guests far more often. "One moment, please. I'll check availability." I clack on my keyboard. "Yes, sir, I've got Penthouse A available. It's a non-smoking suite. Will that work for your client?"

"That's fine."

I describe the basics of the suite and the nightly rate, half expecting the caller to balk when confronted with the outlandish price tag, but nope, he doesn't flinch. "We'll take it," he says without hesitation. "Be there in two minutes."

"Certainly. May I have a name and credit card number to hold the suite, sir? *Sir*?"

But the line is dead.

Damn. It's against company policy for me to hold a room without a name and credit card number. And unfortunately, as I well know after two years of working here, the phrase "be there in two minutes" could mean anything from two minutes to ten hours to not showing up at all. But before I can get too worked up about the situation, a guy whose physical appearance precisely matches the nerdy voice on the phone walks across the lobby and heads straight to the front desk with none other than... Gah! *Lucas Ford* in tow.

Oh my effing God. Lucas Freaking Ford!

I can barely breathe.

My teenage fantasy is now a full-grown man dressed in dark ripped jeans and a tight black T-shirt, an ensemble that perfectly flatters his broad shoulders and muscled physique. His dark hair is tousled like he gives no fucks. And yet, somehow, he looks like he totally meant to do that. The tattoos on his arms are intricate and bold. His cheekbones are striking and his lips kissable. And most heart-stopping of all, his dark eyes—the ones I used to stare into as a teenager while imagining he was my boyfriend doing all manner of naughty things to me—are filled with soul and passion like nothing I've... *Oh.* Wait. Scratch that. Much to my surprise, Lucas Ford's eyes aren't filled with his signature fire tonight. They're blank and lifeless. What the heck? Whenever I've seen Lucas Ford in music videos and doing TV interviews—and especially when I went to his concert so many years ago and beheld his stunning face on a jumbo screen—the unmistakable *passion* in his eyes was by far his most striking feature.

"Hi," the nerdy guy says, drawing my attention away from Lucas Ford, who's drifting toward the far side of the lobby. "I just called about the penthouse?"

I'm dying. I can't believe I'm breathing the same air as Lucas Ford. I take a deep breath and force myself not to completely lose my shit. "Yes, Penthouse A," I manage to say, my voice somehow not betraying my inner freak-out. "May I have a name and credit card, please?" The in-house phone rings. Shit! It's Mr. Seven Oh One again. "Excuse me a moment, sir."

"I'm in a hurry," Nerd Guy says, his tone snippy. "I've got to get my client to his room before fans show up and start demanding fucking selfies." I shift my eyes to Lucas again. He's shuffling toward a grouping of armchairs by the elevator bank, his guitar case in his hand, his head down.

Crap. Where's Danica when I need her? "Of course," I say. "I'll put the caller on hold." I pick up the phone. "Hello, Mr. Anthony. Will you hold a moment, sir?"

"Those bastards are still making noise!" Mr. Seven Oh One shouts into my ear.

"Hold please, sir," I say and quickly push the hold button. I smile at Nerd Guy. "Sorry about that, sir. Now, let's get your client checked in." I can't resist glancing at Lucas Ford across the lobby again, my breathing shallow. He's slumped in a chair by the elevators, his hands over his face, his guitar case leaning against a nearby chair. Oh my God, he looks like a work of art: *Tragically Beautiful Rock Star Reposed in Deep Contemplation.*

Out of nowhere, Danica's standing next to me.

"Room seven oh one is on hold," I mutter to her, relieved she's here. I indicate the flashing red light on the phone.

Danica flashes me a smile that doesn't reach her eyes—a smile that instantly makes it clear to me she hasn't noticed the rock star in our midst on the other end of the lobby. "Perfect," she says in a clipped tone. "I'll handle our guest's check-in while you assist Mr. Anthony. He was asking for you when I went up there a moment ago." She addresses Nerd Guy. "Your identification and credit card, sir? I'll get you checked in right away." In one fell swoop, she rips the keyboard out of my hands, puts her palm out to Nerd Guy, and gets the goods from him, leaving me to handle the guest who's quickly become the bane of both our existences.

Damn, she's good.

I clear my throat and pick up the phone. "Hello, Mr. Anthony. How can I help you?"

Mr. Seven Oh One reads me the riot act about some purported noise at the other end of the seventh floor that Danica apparently didn't resolve adequately for him when she was up there a few moments ago, and I politely promise to come up there immediately to handle the issue.

"I'll be back," I say to no one in particular, walking around the front desk. I make my way toward the elevators. Toward Lucas freaking Ford!

It's harder and harder to breathe with each step I take.

Holy hell, he's larger than life, even just sitting there slumped in a chair.

I'm mere feet away from him now, steps away from the man I've dreamed of kissing since I was fifteen years old.

My legs wobble. I might hyperventilate.

You can do this, Abby. Put one foot in front of the other. Breathe.

I close in on my teenage fantasy and stare at his downturned face, hoping against hope he might *happen* to glance up and catch my eye as I pass. I know it's silly, but I just want to smile at him, just once in my life. And *maybe* even get a return smile from him that I'd surely never forget.

I'm three feet away from him now...and glory be, he's lowering his hands from his face at this very moment! And he's lifting his head...and...Oh my God! *No.* The unthinkable is happening right before my stricken eyes. Lucas Ford is pulling out a cigarette and a lighter...and now he's putting the blasted cigarette between his lips, and...

"I'm sorry, sir, there's no smoking in the lobby," I blurt, stopping and standing right in front of him. Oh, fuck my life. I did *not* just say that to Lucas Ford! And I didn't just use my eighty-year-old-librarian voice when I said it to him, either...right?

At my stern warning, Lucas Ford doesn't even pause. He lights the cigarette dangling precariously between his luscious lips like I hadn't said a damned word.

My heart is beating out of my chest. "I'm sorry, sir," I manage to choke out, my voice trembling. "You can't smoke in the lobby. It's against the law."

Lucas Ford's dark eyes lock with mine. That same blankness I noticed in them before is still eerily present. He takes a long, languid drag on his cigarette and silently blows smoke to the side. "Make an exception."

My heart lurches into my throat. *Lucas Ford just spoke to me!* Of course, this particular conversation is nothing like the one I used to fantasize about having with him if I ever met him. But hey, at least he spoke to me. "Sorry, I can't make an exception," I say, my heart racing. "It's illegal to smoke in a hotel lobby under the Colorado Clean Indoor Air Act of 2006." Oh, Jesus Christ. I did *not* just cite a statute to Lucas Ford! I feel the distinct urge to palm my forehead, but I somehow refrain.

Mr. Rock Star's eyes are dead, dead, dead. He takes another long drag of his cigarette and blows the smoke out in a long, purposeful stream, this time straight at my face. "I think we can safely ignore the Colorado Clean Indoor Air Act of 2006 at three in the morning on a Monday. Don't you think? Let's agree to live dangerously, just this once..."—he glances at my nametag—"*Abby.*"

My entire body's buzzing at the sound of Lucas Ford saying my name—even though, yes, I admit it's not optimal that he said my name with obvious disdain. I take a deep breath and consciously force myself not to kiss my job goodbye and hurl myself at the man like a missile. "I'm sorry, Mr. Ford. If it were up to me, I'd 'live dangerously' with you all night long, but I can't because this job pays my rent, and unfortunately one of my duties is enforcing the rules."

Lucas takes another long drag of his cigarette. "Make a fucking exception, *Abby.*"

Seriously? I put my hands on my hips. "Sorry, I really can't make an exception for you, Mr. Ford. See, that's the crazy thing about laws. They apply at all hours of the day or night, no matter which day of the week it happens to be, and no matter the profession of the lawbreaker." My heart racing, I lean forward and whisper, "Yes, Mr. Ford, the law even applies to rock stars with exceptionally large dicks." I lean away from him and stare him down, feeling equal parts shocked and proud those badass words just escaped my lips.

One side of Mr. Rock Star's mouth tilts up. "Wow," he says. "Abby the Ass-kicker."

I nod curtly. "When I need to be."

He sucks on his cigarette again. "I take it you've seen my sex tape?"

My stomach tightens. "I didn't mean to invade your privacy. Sorry."

"No need to apologize. If I were you, I'd watch it, too." For a long beat, Lucas brazenly looks me up and down like he's deciding whether to purchase me from a pirate-bride auction. "Did you like what you saw in the video, Abby the Ass-kicker?"

Oh, my, my. This conversation seems to be taking a delicious turn. "I liked it a lot, actually."

He leans back in his armchair and takes another long drag of his cigarette. "You a fan of mine?"

I nod. "A big fan."

He sucks on his cigarette again. "How big?"

"I saw your very first tour when I was fifteen. You had to be nineteen or twenty, and when you started playing 'Shattered Hearts,' I burst into tears."

He looks wholly unimpressed, like he's heard the exact same thing a billion times before.

My stomach clenches. "I had a poster of you on my bedroom wall," I add quickly. "I probably listened to 'Shattered Hearts' on a loop for a solid year in my bedroom, staring at your face every single time." My heart is beating wildly. "I'd blare that song late at night and get into bed and..." I abruptly close my mouth. Holy shit, what am I doing? I can't say what I was about to say to this man—especially not at work. I clear my throat and straighten up. "Suffice it to say, I was a big fan."

He bristles. "You *were* a fan? Past tense?"

I feel my cheeks burn. *Shit.* The expression on his face tells me I've messed up. "Oh, no, I'm still a fan of yours. Of course. I'm just not, you know, an obsessive teenager anymore."

He slumps back into his chair, his body language painting the portrait of a man who doesn't give a shit.

Oh, really? I didn't kiss his rock star ass to his liking? I clench my jaw, suddenly feeling a thumping desire to put this entitled asshole in his place. "That's what happens to obsessive teenagers, I guess. They grow up to become adults who have no choice but to enforce the Colorado Clean Indoor Air Act of 2006." I put my hand out and practically tap my toe, my body language telling him in no uncertain terms I'm waiting for him to finally stop acting like a self-entitled douche-canoe and give me his damned cigarette. But he doesn't do it. Nope. The prick just keeps on sucking on his cancer stick, his eyes dead and his body language utterly apathetic. *Un-freaking-believable.* "Look, Mr. Ford," I spit out. "I could get fired if you don't put that thing out." I motion vaguely to the ceiling. "There are video cameras throughout the lobby, and my boss might be watching. So, please, do me a huge favor and stop acting like a rock star cliché for thirty seconds and give me your damned cigarette."

Okay, yeah, I'm pouring it on a bit thick, not to mention bullshitting about my job being on the line here. I mean, yes, there are video cameras in the lobby—that part is true—but it's highly unlikely anyone other than the security guy is watching, and he certainly doesn't have authority to fire me. But still, Lucas Ford's being an entitled asshole right now, and that makes me want to knock the cocky bastard down a peg or two or three.

Lucas takes another long suck on his cigarette, quite plainly telling me he doesn't give a fuck if the poor little hotel clerk loses her job because of him.

Okay, now I'm pissed. Smoking a stupid cigarette at three in the morning in a hotel lobby is more important to him than my livelihood? What an asshole! What a sexy motherfucking bad-boy asshole with a big dick! Oh, Jesus. My clit is pounding like a jackhammer, even as my blood is simmering with near-homicidal rage.

I put my hand out to him, my eyes locked onto his. "Give me the *fucking* cigarette, *Mr. Ford.*" I lean in close enough to catch a whiff of his deliciously masculine scent and whisper into his ear. "I'm not fucking around here, *sir*. Last chance to prove you're a decent human being, or else, if there's a hell, I'm sure you'll be going to it."

I pull back and glare at him, and when I do, I'm surprised to find his eyes flickering with unmistakable heat.

Lucas bites his luscious lip. "How the hell can a woman who looks so much like a kindergarten teacher kick so much ass?"

I shrug. "Don't judge a book by its cover. I assure you I'm the last woman in the world who's going to read you *Goodnight Moon.*"

He can't help himself. He throws his head back and laughs out loud, and the sound of his sexy laughter sends heat flashing through my core.

I put out my hand, sighing. "Just give me the damned cigarette, Mr. Ford. For the love of God. Enough with the rock star attitude. I'm tired."

A heart-stopping smile spreads across his beautiful face. And finally, slowly, *blessedly,* the bastard hands me his damned cigarette.

I take the contraband from him and immediately adopt a prim, professional affect. "Thank you, Mr. Ford. Welcome to The Rockford, sir."

He licks his lips in a decidedly sexual way. "Please, don't call me Mr. Ford. I'm Lucas or Luke." He leans forward like he's telling me a secret. "And don't call me 'sir.' Unless, of course, I happen to be fucking you. In which case, please do."

My lips part in surprise.

He smirks, his formerly dead eyes positively on fire now.

I clear my throat. "I'll keep that in mind—if ever you're lucky enough to be fucking me."

Oh, man, those eyes of his are a five-alarm fire now. He opens his mouth to say something, but Nerd Guy appears and cuts him off.

"Come on, Luke," Nerd Guy says, traipsing toward the elevators. He indicates the lit cigarette in my hand. "Is that yours? *Dude.* How many times have I told you? You can't smoke in hotel lobbies in Colorado. There's a law."

"Yeah, so this lovely woman was just explaining to me." He stands and gathers his guitar case. "See ya 'round, Abby the Ass-kicker. Thanks for the legal education. It was highly entertaining."

"My pleasure, *sir*. It's been my pleasure to properly welcome you to our fine hotel." I smile at him sweetly and Mr. Dead Eyes surprises me by winking at me in reply.

The minute the elevator doors close behind Lucas and his handler, I crumple into the armchair Lucas vacated mere seconds ago, the dwindling remnants of his cigarette still lodged between my index finger and thumb.

Oh my gosh. That was the most exciting thing that's ever happened to me in my entire life. Who was I just now? I can't believe the things I said to him...and, even more so, the things I *implied.* It was like I was a sexy heroine from a James Bond movie! My fifteen-year-old self would be high-fiving me right now, and, I must admit, I'd be high-fiving her right back.

I look down at the burning cigarette in my shaking hand, my heart and clit both raging. Even though I know I should snuff the thing out, I can't seem to do it. Not yet, anyway. Instead, I turn my back on the video camera affixed to the ceiling above me, place my mouth around the end of the cigarette, wrapping my lips around the exact spot where Lucas Ford's lips rested moments ago. And I give that motherfucker a good, long *suck*...imagining, as I do, quite graphically, that I'm sucking on Lucas Ford's gigantic throbbing cock until his warm liquid magic is shooting straight down my hungry throat.

CHAPTER THREE

"Oh my fucking God!" Danica whispers. "That was *him*? How did I not see him sitting over there? And you were *talking* to him?"

"Yeah, he lit a cigarette and I told him—"

The phone rings and the display screen tells us it's the guest in Penthouse A.

"It's *him*!" Danica squeals. She grabs the phone before I can even think to reach for it. "Hello, sir, how can I help you?" She pauses. "No, this is Danica. The one with the dark hair who was standing behind the front desk."

I bristle. Of course, Danica wants Lucas Ford to know she's the hot brunette behind the front desk and not the dirty-blond plain-Jane kindergarten teacher who berated him about the freaking Colorado Clean Indoor Air Act of 2006. Because, as Danica knows full well, any man in the world—including a world-famous rock star—would be attracted to her over me. Because unlike me, Danica Reynolds is just plain sexy, no matter what she does or wears or says. No impersonation of a *femme fatale* in a James Bond movie required.

Danica continues talking into the phone, a smile plastered across her face. "I'd certainly be thrilled to help you with whatever you require, Mr. Ford." Her smile vanishes. "Oh. Sure thing." She holds the phone out to me, her eyes like daggers. "Mr. Ford says he wants to talk to 'Abby the Ass-kicker.'"

My heart lurches. I grab the phone from Danica, my heart in my throat. "This is Abby."

"Is this Colorado's foremost expert on the Indoor Clean Air Act of 2006?"

My heart skips a beat. "Yes, it is. Actually, I'll be teaching a seminar on the finer points of the statute in the fourth-floor conference room later. Oh, and I'm going to close out my lecture with a reading of *Goodnight Moon.*"

I can hear his smile across the phone line.

"You should come down and check it out, *sir,*" I add. "It's going to be a fantastically good time."

Lucas chuckles. "I've actually got a much better idea. Why don't you come up to my suite for an even better *fantastically good time*? You can teach me about any Colorado statute you like, one-on-one."

Blood whooshes into my crotch. I open my mouth and abruptly close it again, incapable of replying. Did Lucas Ford just invite me up to his room for sex? That's what he meant, right? "I'm, uh, working," I say lamely.

"Ah, that's right. A working girl. Well, is the kitchen open? Consider this my call to order room service. Actually, that's a good idea. I'm starving."

I shift my eyes to Danica. She's staring at me like I have three heads.

I clear my throat. "Yes, sir, a limited version of the menu is available during off-hours. Would you like me to connect you with room service so they can tell you what's available?"

"No, I'd strongly prefer to have an ass-kicker order a bunch of different things plus a bottle of Jim Beam and bring me everything herself."

I think I'm going to have a heart attack. "Sure. I'd be happy to assist you with that, sir." I glance at Danica again and she looks like she's about to have a stroke.

Three women enter the lobby, laughing at the tops of their lungs, and one of them beelines to Danica and begins asking her something about bus routes.

I turn my back on Danica and the woman and whisper into the phone. "What would you like me to bring you, Mr. Ford?"

"Lucas, remember? Just bring me whatever you like and make it two. It's time for you to take your lunch break, Abby."

Oh, jeez, I feel like I'm going to pass out. I know I talked a good game earlier when Lucas was acting like a douche, but now that he's seemingly hitting on me, I'm feeling like I might be in over my head here. I haven't gone fishing for a bad boy in five years, and I'm quite certain I'm waaaay out of practice. And waaaay out of my league. I mean, seriously, this guy's not a bad-boy fish, he's a freaking whale. "What about your friend?" I whisper into the phone, my back still facing Danica. "Would he like something to eat, too?"

But I'm talking to no one. The line is dead.

I stare at the phone for a moment in disbelief and finally return it to its cradle.

"What'd he say?" Danica asks, her eyes as big as saucers.

I glance across the lobby and locate the trio of women heading toward the elevators.

"Uh, nothing much," I say. "He said he's hungry." I tell Danica a watered-down version of what Lucas Ford said to me and she pouts.

"Why'd he ask *you* to bring his food?" she says. "No offense, but you look like you're going to sit him down and try to sell him insurance."

I chuckle. She's right. I totally do. "I have no idea why me. Maybe he just wants to tell me off for making him put out his cigarette?"

Danica practically stomps her foot with frustration. "Why couldn't *I* have been the one standing here when Lucas Ford came in? One look at me and my body made for sin and he'd have known right away I'd suck his dick. I mean, no offense, honey, but if he wants a woman who's going to help him blow off a little steam after a hard night at the arena, and not one who's going to sit him down and try to sell him an annuity, then clearly I'm his girl."

I chuckle. "Don't worry, Dani. All's right with the world. There's no way Lucas Ford is going to hit on me, even if he wanted to—which he doesn't. His friend is still up there with him, remember? Nothing too exciting could possibly happen with that guy still there. I'm just going to bring Mr. Rock Star a sandwich and tell him how amazing he is and that will be that."

"Yeah, I know, but still, I'm totally jealous."

"Don't be. Nothing could happen with Nerd Guy still—"

One of the elevator's doors open and Lucas Ford's handler enters the lobby...

Frozen, Danica and I watch him stride past us and straight out the front door of the hotel without a backward glance.

CHAPTER FOUR

I rap on the door to Penthouse A, my body trembling with anticipation.

"Just breathe, Abby," I whisper under my breath, my eyes trained on the closed door, my heartbeat thudding in my ears. "He's a human being, just like anyone else."

But the door's not opening.

I shift my weight. Force air into my lungs. Wipe my sweaty palms on the front of my skirt.

Did he not hear me knock?

I raise my fist to rap on the door a second time at the precise moment it cracks open. And there he is in the doorway. My teenage fantasy. Shirtless, all grown-up, and looking sexy as hell.

"Mr. Ford," I squeak out, my throat tight.

"Lucas." He widens the door to let me pass. On wobbly legs, I push the food cart into the room and straight toward a small table on the other side of the large living area.

When I reach the table, I turn around, expecting Lucas to be standing behind me. But he hasn't followed me. He's settled himself onto a black leather couch on the other side of the room, his legs spread wide and his eight-pack abs on mesmerizing display.

"Would you prefer the food over there on the coffee table, sir?"

I ask.

"What'd I tell you about calling me sir?"

"Sorry. Force of habit." I bring the bottle of Jim Beam and a couple plates to the coffee table and stand awkwardly over him, not sure if I should leave or sit.

"Sit," he commands, reading my mind.

I sit.

Lucas motions to the bottle of bourbon. "Have a drink with me."

"I really shouldn't. I'm working."

"One."

"Okay."

He smirks. "Well, that was easy."

Shoot. He's right. That was way too easy. I need to pull myself together and pretend to be a *femme fatale* in a James Bond movie again.

Lucas grabs the bottle of bourbon, takes a long swig, and hands it to me.

I take a little sip, giddy to be sharing a bottle with him, and hand it back to him.

He pulls out a box of cigarettes and offers it to me.

"This is a non-smoking room, actually," I say, and the minute the words come out I want to stuff them back in.

Lucas smirks. "God help us if we violate the Colorado Clean Indoor Air Act of 2007 *again*."

"2006. And it doesn't apply here. It's just a designated non-smoking suite."

"Ah. Well, then, sounds like I can risk it." He slides a cigarette between his beautiful lips and lights it. "So you said you're a big fan of mine?" He exhales a huge plume of smoke.

I try not to cough. "I am. 'Shattered Hearts' is one of my all-time favorite songs."

"Yeah, that's everyone's favorite, isn't it?"

My stomach tightens at his caustic tone.

"What about my new stuff?" he asks, taking another hit of his cigarette. "What's your favorite song off my last album?"

Oh, shit. I didn't buy his last album. I search my memory for whatever song from it played on an endless loop on the radio, but I can't think of a single one.

"I, uh, haven't been listening to a whole lot of music these past two years," I confess. "I've been in law school part-time, plus working here and studying or sleeping every free minute."

"My last album came out three years ago," he says, his eyes hard. "Were you in law school three years ago?"

I feel my cheeks rise with color. "No."

"Working here?"

"No."

His eyes drift from my face down my body and back up to my face. "Feel free to take that blazer off," he says. "It's warm in here."

It's not warm in here. In fact, it's a bit chilly. But I stand and take my blazer off, anyway. I lay the blazer across the back of my chair, and then smooth my shirt and skirt a bit, emphasizing the lines of my taut body for him, and sit again.

Lucas takes another swig of his bourbon, still looking me up and down, but he doesn't speak. Damn. His eyes are dead again. Dead, dead, dead.

"Is your friend coming back?" I ask, fidgeting with the hem of my skirt.

"He's not my friend. He's my warden. And no, he's not coming back."

I wait, expecting him to say more—maybe to explain his "warden" comment—but he doesn't. I push a lock of my dirty-blond hair behind my ear and clear my throat, still waiting.

But Lucas doesn't speak. He takes another sip of bourbon, seemingly lost in his thoughts.

After a moment of awkward silence, my stomach growls embarrassingly and I look at the food on the coffee table, wondering if it would be appropriate for me to take a big ol' bite of one of the BLTs.

"So what'd you think of the video, Abby?" he finally says, filling the silence.

"The music video for 'Shattered Hearts'? I loved it."

He smiles. "No. The video making the rounds all over the internet right now. The one of me having sex."

My chest tightens. "Oh. I...I thought it was really...impressive."

One side of his mouth tilts up. "Did you see the edited or unedited version?"

My face is hot. I swallow hard. "I don't know. How would I know which one I saw?"

He takes a long drag on his cigarette. "Well, did you see me come all over her tits at the end or not?"

I widen my eyes, and open and close my mouth.

He smirks. "I can see by your facial expression you saw the *edited* version." He takes another swig from his bottle. "Did you like what you saw?"

"I, um..." I swallow hard again. "To be honest, I felt like I was invading your privacy." I take a deep breath. "I couldn't help thinking it was pretty disgusting of your girlfriend to leak the video without your permission."

"She isn't my girlfriend and it wasn't without my permission," he says matter-of-factly. "So, tell me, do you have any interest in seeing the *unedited* version?"

Holy shit. Is he offering to show me the *actual* unedited video or was that his coded way of asking me if I'd like him to come all over my tits? I stare at him blankly, feeling like I'm short-circuiting. This guy has been my sexual fantasy for as long I can remember. He's my Desert Island Fantasy, for crying out loud. But now that I'm sitting here in the real world, I'm not sure how far I'm willing to take this flirtation. Would I truly go all the way with this man, this fast, simply because he's Lucas Ford? I'm a bit overwhelmed. I thought I was coming up here to eat a sandwich and maybe flirt with him for a bit and then—*perhaps*—after some laughter and butterflies and some good-old-fashioned seduction by Mr. Rock Star, I'd *maybe* fuck him if I were *really* feeling it. But does he truly think he need only snap his fingers and I'll spread my legs for him? Is it always just that easy for him to get laid by strangers? As easy as buying a turkey sandwich at a deli?

Speaking of sandwiches...oh, man, my stomach just growled again.

I open my mouth to ask him for clarification of his question about the video—or inquire if now would be a good time for us to eat our BLTs—but he lets out a long and exhausted-sounding exhale that instantly shuts me up.

"So, are we going to fuck or not, Ass-kicker?" he asks, his tone full of impatience. He looks at his watch and sighs dramatically like I'm taking up his valuable time. "'Cause if you didn't come up here to fuck me, I've got to move on to drinking myself into oblivion and start writing a stupid fucking song about heartbreak for the cocksuckers at my label."

I bolt to standing, too shocked and mortified to sit still. He expects me to spread my legs for him after talking to me like that?

Lucas chuckles. "Yeah, that's what I thought, *Ass-kicker*. Your mouth wrote a check your body can't cash." He flicks the ashes of his cigarette onto the sandwich he told me to order for myself, completely ruining it, and flashes me a hard smile that doesn't reach his eyes. "I guess you're not quite the ass-kicker you were pretending to be, huh?" He motions to the door like he's done with me. "Bye, sweetheart."

I grit my teeth. "Oh, I'm an ass-kicker, all right," I say, rage welling up inside me. "I just don't happen to be a *whore*."

He calmly sucks on his cigarette, his eyes dead as can be.

Shame is slamming into me. I can't believe I've loved this ogre for almost ten years. I can't believe I came in here thinking I was going to get to eat a sandwich with my rock star fantasy while fangirling all over him and asking him a bunch of stupid questions about his songwriting process and inspirations and band. And after that, if the vibe was right, if he was as sexy and swoon worthy as his music videos and interviews and lyrics make him out to be, that I was *maybe* going to throw caution and my panties to the wind and break all my hard-and-fast rules and screw him to within an inch of his life, just to say I did. But clearly, that's not going to happen now. Hell no. In fact, I can honestly say this boorish rock star is the last man on earth I'd have sex with at this point.

My face burning, I march toward the door of the suite and grab the door handle. But before I turn it, I realize I'll regret stalking out of here without giving this asshole a piece of my mind. I whirl around, my chest heaving, to find him still sitting on the couch, calmly swigging his bottle of booze like he hasn't just stabbed his biggest fan in her heart.

"I can't believe you're the same man who wrote 'Shattered Hearts'!" I shout, barely able to keep myself from crying. "Did someone ghostwrite that song for you? Because it's awfully hard to believe those passionate, beautiful lyrics came out of a soulless prick like you!"

I whirl around toward the door again and grab the handle but quickly realize I'm not even close to finished with him yet.

I spin around again. "You think being a rock star gives you the right to treat women like paid whores who refuse to swallow?"

Lucas cocks his head to the side, obviously surprised by my choice of words.

"I heard you had a bad time at your concert tonight. And I'm sorry for whatever's going on in your life that's making you act like the world's biggest douche." I put my hands on my hips. "But guess what, asshole? You're not the only human on this planet with talent and you're most certainly not the only one with problems. Some of us have to work really hard for a living on the freaking night shift while also going to law school part-time so after graduation they can land a job they don't even want. Some of us are living paycheck to paycheck trying to make ends meet, trying to have a healthy, productive life despite past screw-ups. And some of us would have really appreciated a free goddamned sandwich, not to mention getting to share that free sandwich with their teenage fantasy!" Oh, man, I'm on a roll and I'm not stopping now. "Would it have killed you to be charming to a woman before demanding she fuck you? Would it have killed you to say, 'So where ya from, Abby?' or 'Tell me a bit about yourself, Abby,' or 'What are your goals and ambitions, Abby?' Or maybe something as simple as, 'What's your favorite color, Abby?' Or jeez, I don't know, would it have *killed* you to let me ask some cliché and annoying fangirl questions, even if you get asked them all the time, like, 'What's the story behind 'Shattered Hearts'?' Honestly, would that have *killed* you, Lucas Fucking Ford?"

If I'm not mistaken, Lucas's eyes are flickering with heat.

"Honestly, it boggles my mind you messed this up," I continue. "If anyone in the world was going to come up here and agree to have sex with you, it was me. I gave myself my first orgasm at fifteen while listening to 'Shattered Hearts' while staring at a poster of you on my wall. And for years after that, I got myself off infinite times imagining I was giving you the most amazing blowjob of your life or that you were eating me out or fucking me. But what I didn't consciously realize until just now was that those fantasies all included the baseline assumption that you weren't a total and complete asshole."

Lucas subtly bites his lower lip.

"Honestly, if you must know, you needed a written book of instructions on how not to get laid by me," I continue. "That stupid sex tape of yours had me all primed and ready for you, if only you'd been the slightest bit charming to me. Oh my God, that video! I've watched it on a running loop. And you want to know what turned me on the most? It wasn't your big dick. Or even the way you gripped her hair. It was the way you looked straight into the camera while screwing her. Because that told me you're a bit of a dirty motherfucker. And guess what? *I secretly like dirty motherfuckers.*"

Lucas's eyebrows shoot up.

"I can't believe how *little* I want to have sex with you right now, given what your sex tape did to me. After watching it here at work for the first time, I was so turned on I marched straight into a restroom and fingered my aching clit for no more than fifteen seconds before I came like a freaking freight train, all the while imagining I was fucking you like an animal. But now that I know the truth about you? Ha! I don't want to touch your big dick with a ten-foot pole. And you know why? Because I don't fuck flaming assholes!"

I whirl around, swing the heavy door to the suite open, and march through it without so much as a backward glance.

I reach the elevator at the end of the hallway, shaking with rage and hurt and shame. I bang on the call button furiously while stealing glances at the door of the penthouse, half expecting Lucas to burst out and beg me to wait a minute so he can apologize.

But Lucas doesn't appear.

The door to the penthouse remains firmly closed.

And now I feel doubly stupid for thinking my words might actually have made an impact on Mr. Rock Star.

God, I'm such a fool! How did I let myself feel so much love for Lucas Ford over the years? He's not the man his music makes him out to be. In fact, he's a total and complete fraud.

The doors to the elevator open and I step inside. And the minute the doors close again, I cover my face and burst into big, soggy tears.

CHAPTER FIVE

I take a few minutes to compose myself and wash my face in the bathroom, and slip stoically behind the front desk, my heart aching.

"So?" Danica asks brightly.

"So, nothing," I mumble. I clack on the keyboard and bring up a template for P&R reports, intending to get started on my work.

Danica stares at me, obviously waiting for me to say more.

But I don't.

"What happened with Lucas Ford?" she blurts.

"Nothing. I brought him some food. We talked for two minutes about how amazing he is, and then I left. He's actually a huge prick, to be honest."

"He didn't hit on you?"

"Nope."

Danica sighs with relief. "I can't say I'm surprised. From what I've seen on celebrity gossip sites, you're definitely not his type. He tends to go for Playboy Bunny types like that blonde with the jugs in the video. No offense, but I'm guessing you'd need to add at least three cup sizes to catch that man's attention."

"No offense taken. I'm glad I'm not his type. Like I said, he's a prick."

"Jeez, Abby, what the hell did he say to you? I thought you said you talked to him for two minutes."

"I did. And in that short time he made it abundantly clear he thinks he's God's gift to the world."

"Well, to be fair, he is."

"He's a prick, Dani, plain and simple. I don't care how famous he is. He still needs to behave like a decent human being."

"Did he say why he asked you to personally bring his food? If he didn't hit on you, then I don't get the point."

"I'm sure he was just throwing a tantrum. You know, trying to inconvenience me. I'm the girl who told the gilded rock star not to smoke in the lobby, after all. *Gasp*. He obviously thought demanding the bitchy front desk clerk be the one to personally bring him food would feel demeaning to me."

"I bring food to guests all the time when the kitchen is short-staffed or whatever."

"Yeah, so do I. But he doesn't know that." I wave dismissively in the air. "Just forget it. I don't have any idea what he was thinking, and I don't want to know."

Danica shrugs. "I wouldn't take his tantrum personally. I think he's in the midst of some sort of personal crisis. His handler said he's going to be writing up there this entire week without leaving the building. I got the feeling Lucas has no choice in the matter. Isn't that kind of weird?"

"I have no idea what's normal in the music industry."

"Oh, by the way, the nerdy guy said Lucas is a real night owl. Up all night, sleeps all day. The guy said we should check in with Lucas around the start of our shift every night just to make sure he's eating something. Apparently, lots of artists forget to eat or drink when

MISADVENTURES ON THE NIGHT SHIFT

they're doing a marathon writing session."

"Then let's not check up on him. If we're lucky, maybe he'll forget to eat and drink and drop dead."

"Jesus, Abby, what on earth did he say to you up there?"

"He was just rude, that's all."

"Note to self. Never be rude to Abby Medford or she'll leave you to starve to death." She giggles. "Hey, let me be the one who brings him food tomorrow night, okay? You've had your chance to seduce him."

"Be my guest. I'm not working tomorrow night, anyway. But if I were, I'd say, 'He's all yours.'"

"God, he really must have been a jerk to you. I thought you absolutely loved Lucas Ford?"

"I did. But not anymore. I'll never hear his songs the same way again. In fact, I never want to hear another one of his stupid songs, period."

Danica rolls her eyes. "Come on, Abby. You're the one who told him he couldn't smoke at three in the morning in an empty lobby... right after he'd had some sort of meltdown at his concert. I bet he'll be a lot less rude to *me* when I go up there with some food and make it abundantly clear I'm up for anything, unlike Little Miss Girl Scout Cigarette Police." She snorts.

I pull the keyboard toward me. "Like I said, he's all yours." I focus on the computer, my brow furrowed, and begin working on the P&R reports, telling myself I'm never going to speak to that asshole again, or listen to one of his songs, or fantasize about him, or watch that sexy-as-hell sex tape, or drool over any of his music videos, or...

"Hey, Abby," Danica says, drawing me out of my rambling,

murderous, boycotting thoughts.

I look up from the computer.

"Where's your blazer?" she asks. "I could have sworn you were wearing it when you got here."

I look down at myself and instantly remember the whereabouts of my stupid traitor of a blazer. I close my eyes and exhale. "*Shit.*"

CHAPTER SIX

I'm trying to concentrate on what the professor is saying at the front of the classroom, but I can't. I'm too wound up by what happened earlier this morning at the hotel. I can't believe Lucas Ford turned out to be a narcissistic, asshole douche. And I can't believe I told him off! He's a VIP guest in our most expensive penthouse suite, after all. What the heck is wrong with me?

I hope I have a job waiting for me when I go back to work. I think the odds are fifty-fifty he's going to get me fired. Obviously, he won't tell my boss the truth about our exchange, but he could easily think of something horrible to say about me to get me fired if he were feeling particularly vindictive.

And then where would I find another night job that pays as well as The Rockford and allows me to sneak in two to three solid hours of studying every shift before racing here to school to sit through two morning classes? Shoot. Maybe I should have just screwed the guy, asshat or not. I mean, at least it would have been something to check off my bucket list, right? A story to tell at cocktail parties. Not that I ever go to cocktail parties. Wow. I had no idea I'd developed so much self-respect over the past five years. *Thanks, Dr. Carlson! You'd be so proud of me if you knew!*

"What do you think, Miss Medford?" my professor asks,

drawing me out of my thoughts.

"I...uh," I stammer. "I'm sorry, Professor. I was daydreaming." I flash him a genuinely apologetic look.

My professor smiles. He knows I work the night shift at a downtown hotel and that I'm working my ass off to make this crazy schedule of mine work. "It happens to the best of us," he says kindly. He scans the crowd for his next victim and focuses on a handsome guy in the front row named Noah. "Mr. Endicott?" my professor asks. "Can you tell us about the court's rationale in this case?"

Noah answers the professor's question with aplomb and I zone out again, letting my mind wander to a thousand thoughts, all of them having to do with Lucas Ford.

Finally, the class ends and I begin gathering my laptop and books, my mind and body both exhausted from the mental and physical toll of the past several hours.

"Hey, Abby."

I look up. It's Noah, the guy the professor called on earlier. He's always flirting with me, even though to my knowledge I've never done anything to encourage him. Yes, he's handsome, but he's far too straitlaced for my taste.

"Hi, Noah," I reply.

Noah's wide smile reveals straight, white teeth. "I'm having a little party tonight. A small group is gonna watch the game and have pizza, and play beer pong or Cards Against Humanity or whatever. I was hoping you could make it?"

I pause. Noah's definitely cute. And his body is really attractive. True, he seems a bit stodgy for my taste, but maybe that's exactly the kind of guy I should be pursuing nowadays. Maybe the way I reacted to Lucas Ford's behavior earlier this morning is proof, once and for all, I'm *finally* ready to move on from bad boys and act like a mature and reasonable grown-up when it comes to romance. "Tonight just so happens to be my night off," I say brightly to Noah. "I'd love to come."

Noah's smile lights up his entire face. "What's your number? I'll text you the address."

I give him my number and he texts me the information.

"And hey, if you want to bring your toothbrush and a change of clothes or whatever, that's cool," he says. "That way you can drink as much as you want and crash." His face flushes. "On my couch, I mean. Or I could sleep on my couch and you could take my bed. Whatever works."

"Thanks," I say, doing my best to suppress my amusement at his sudden awkwardness. "That's really sweet but not necessary. If I drink, I'll just Uber home."

Noah nods, disappointment washing over his face. "Yeah, of course. I didn't mean to imply any expectation... I just meant, you know, just in case."

I resist the urge to sigh audibly. Damn. It would have been so much better if he hadn't back-pedaled. If he'd acted like it was a foregone conclusion he was going to seduce me tonight because he's just that good. Out of nowhere, I think of Lucas Ford's sexy voice saying, *"Don't call me sir...unless I happen to be fucking you."* And my clit pulses at the delicious memory. Why can't Noah be more like Lucas Ford? Lucas might be a douche, but at least he's a sexy one. I clear my throat and smile kindly at Noah. "No worries. I know exactly what you meant and I appreciate your thoughtfulness. It was sweet of you to think of my safety. I'll see you tonight."

CHAPTER SEVEN

Noah's lips are on mine. His hand is on my breast. His hard-on is jutting into my crotch.

We're standing on the balcony of Noah's apartment as a small group of people plays beer pong inside, and his breath on my skin feels especially warm in the cool night air.

Noah's not a bad kisser, actually. Better than I thought he'd be. And now that he's wrapping his arms around me and pressing his body against mine, I can plainly surmise he's got a really fit body underneath his sweater and jeans. Not too shabby for a future lawyer. Plus, he's definitely on track to make a mighty fine living one day, so that's a plus. As my mother always says, it's just as easy to fall in love with a rich boy as a poor one. Yep, by all measures, Noah's a good catch.

And yet, I'm not feeling it at all.

The way Noah's kissing me isn't even in the stratosphere of the way I need to be kissed to want to have sex with someone. Honestly, the minute he started kissing me, I knew in my bones he could fuck me with everything he's got—and throw in a vibrating dildo, to boot—and I'd literally yawn and start thinking about my grocery list.

Yeah, this is a no-go.

I pull out of our kiss and push gently on Noah's chest. "Sorry,"

I breathe, wiping my mouth. "I don't think this is going to work out, Noah."

Noah looks stricken. "What do you mean? We can take it slow if you want. However slow you need to take it."

I suppress the urge to smirk. If I had any doubts about Noah Endicott not being my type, he just confirmed it. Poor guy. He's the kind of guy who thinks I want to take it slow when I'm actually aching for him to muster the balls to rip my clothes off and fuck me so hard I'm screaming his name. "It's not you," I lie. "I just got out of a relationship, and I just realized I'm not ready to date again. Sorry. I didn't mean to be a tease. It took me kissing you to fully realize where my head and heart are at."

Noah takes a deep breath. "I understand. No worries. Whenever you're ready to jump in again, just let me know. Standing offer."

"Thanks, Noah. You're a sweetheart."

We stare at each other blankly for an awkward half-beat.

"Well, I guess I'd better go," I finally say.

Twenty minutes later...

I practically sprint through the door of my apartment, grab my laptop and headphones, and careen into my bedroom. Without a moment's hesitation, I strip off my clothes, hop into bed with a bottle of lube, my vibrator, and "Shattered Hearts" blaring into my ears. I furiously search the internet for the unedited version of Lucas's already infamous sex tape, but it's nowhere to be found. Every site that claims to have it shows an error message when I click on the link. *Damn.*

Finally, when my throbbing clit won't be ignored a moment longer, I begrudgingly click on a link promising the edited version of the video. I watch with my vibrator pressed firmly against my tip on the lowest possible setting, intending to prolong my arousal as long as humanly possible. But my body is too wound up to hold off. In less than a minute, I come...so damned hard, in fact, I leave a massive wet splotch underneath me on my sheets.

CHAPTER EIGHT

After an unusually high volume of late-night check-ins and noise complaints and other assorted first-world fiascos, Danica and I have finally reached The Dead Zone.

"So, did Mr. Rock Star hit on you when you brought him food last night?" I ask.

"Nope," Danica replies. "He didn't hit on me at all. And not only that, at the beginning of the shift he called down asking for *you.*"

I smile broadly. Is it wrong everything Danica just said thrilled me? "What'd you tell him when he asked for me?"

"I told him you were off for the night but that you were scheduled to work tonight."

"And then what happened?" I ask.

"He asked for food to be sent up. I tried to flirt with him during the call, but he'd already hung up. And when I went to his room with his food, he barely looked at me. God, I was so bummed. I mean, I knew—" She abruptly smashes her lips together. A man and woman dressed in eveningwear cross the lobby, arm in arm, looking like they're ready to go upstairs and maul each other.

"You knew...?" I prompt after the couple has disappeared into an elevator.

"I knew he didn't come onto *you,*" she whispers. "But I just figured that's because you're *you*. I mean, no offense, but you look like you're going to sell him Thin Mints."

"No offense taken. I love Thin Mints."

"I never thought for a minute he wouldn't hit on me," Danica says, pouting. "I mean, look at me!" She motions to her slammin' body. "Nobody's thinking about Thin Mints when they look at *this*." She sighs. "It just makes no sense. I know his reputation. It's well known he screws a different woman after every concert. And yet, when I got up there with his food he barely looked up from his guitar."

"Oh, well, I'm sure it's nothing personal. The other night, he mentioned he had to write a 'stupid fucking song for his label.' I'm sure he's just stressed out."

Danica pouts. "Well, if he's stressed out, I've got his stress-relief right here, baby." She smacks her own ass. "Maybe the next time I bring him food, I'll—" She abruptly stops talking again, this time because a woman in pajamas and bedhead is approaching the front desk.

"Yes, ma'am?" I ask politely. Oh jeez, the poor thing looks like a shit sandwich.

"Could I get some ibuprofen, please?" the woman chokes out, a pained expression on her face. "I've got a terrible headache and I forgot to pack my migraine medication."

I quickly take care of the woman, and the minute she's dragged her poor ass back onto an elevator, Danica continues talking again.

"Next time I go up there with food," she whispers, "what if I say, 'Hello, Mr. Ford, I'm Danica and I'm here to serve you *in any way you'd like.*'" She imbues those last words with unmistakable innuendo. "What do I have to lose?"

"Your job?" I reply. "Your self-respect?"

Danica makes a face that tells me she doesn't value either of those things more than the chance to have sex with Lucas Ford, but before she can say anything about that, the light on the phone panel flickers, signaling we've got an in-house call...from none other than the guest in Penthouse A.

"Speak of the devil," I say. "Now's your chance to tell Mr. Ford you're here to 'serve' him."

Danica motions for me to pick up the line. "He's just going to ask for you again."

"No, he won't. He only asked for me the other night because I left my blazer in his room."

Danica's face lights up. "Well, why didn't you say so? Ha!" She greedily picks up the phone. "Good evening, Mr. Ford. No, this is *Danica*. The brunette who brought you food last night?" Her smile falls. "Yes, Abby's standing right here. But if this is about her blazer, I'd be happy to..." Danica's face morphs into a full-blown scowl. "Yes, of course." She holds the phone out to me, her eyes hard. "He wants to speak to you."

I don't look up from the computer. "No, thank you."

"Huh?"

"I've got reports to write and I don't want to talk to him."

"*Abby*."

"Tell him I said, 'No, thank you.' Or, hell, tell him I said, 'Go fuck yourself, asshole.'"

Danica's jaw drops. She stares at me for a while before putting the phone to her ear. "I'm sorry, Mr. Ford. Abby's occupied with something. Can I take a message and have her call you back?" She listens. "Yes, sir, she's standing right here, but she's... Okay." She puts the phone to her chest. "He says he has your blazer and now would be an excellent time for you to come get it."

"Please tell Mr. Ford I said, 'Thank you for your offer, *sir*, but I'd rather send housekeeping to retrieve my blazer than come up personally.'"

Danica looks positively floored. "Abby Medford, what's wrong with you?" She stares at me for a long moment, the phone pressed against her chest.

"If you love me at all, tell that man what I said, word for word," I say evenly. "I promise you won't get in trouble."

Danica stares at me again, obviously considering what to do. I say nothing more, and my darling friend puts the phone to her ear and repeats everything I said, word for word, God bless her. When she's finished talking, she listens for a long beat and then says, "Sure thing, sir. One moment." She looks at me, obviously flabbergasted. "Mr. Ford said, 'Fuck the blazer. Tell that stubborn woman to get her ass up to my suite right fucking now. And tell her that's an order from a VIP guest of your fucking hotel.' And then he slammed the phone down."

Oh, jeez. My clit is vibrating. My nipples are hard. The devil sitting on my left shoulder has not only knocked off the angel sitting on my right, she's now stroking her tiny devilish clit with firm, confident strokes. "Call him back and tell him, 'Abby says she has more important things to do than go to the hotel room of an egotistical rock star who doesn't know how to treat women like human beings.' And also tell him, 'She says she couldn't care less if you're a VIP guest. You can go fuck yourself, regardless.'"

Danica gasps. "Abby, you're going too far. I can't say any of that to Lucas Ford or any other guest, especially a VIP like him. Have you lost your mind?"

"Call him and tell him what I said, Dani. Word for word."

"What's going on? You said nothing happened when you went up to his room."

"Nothing did."

"Well, then, what's your deal? Was your ego bruised that your teenage crush didn't hit on you? Is that it?" She looks at me sympathetically. "Abby, come on. He's *Lucas Ford*. He dates boobalicious models and actresses and makes sex tapes with them. You're really pretty, honey, don't get me wrong, but in an Emma-Stone's-kid-sister-who-sells-insurance-and-Girl-Scout-cookies sort of way. Some guys *love* that kind of fresh-faced girl, but that's obviously not his thing." She grins. "I must say, though, I'm impressed you gave it the ol' college try by leaving your blazer in his room. I didn't know you had it in you to pull a stunt like that."

"I didn't leave my blazer in his room on purpose," I say. "And I'm well aware I'm not that bastard's physical type, trust me."

"Then what happened to get you so riled up?"

"He was just incredibly rude to me, that's all. Even if he's not attracted to me, he didn't have to treat me like shit. Now please, call him and tell him I don't want to talk to him. Do this for me, honey. Please. Do it for womankind. I promise you won't get into trouble."

Danica rolls her eyes like she's dealing with an insane lunatic, but she nonetheless grants my request. She picks up the phone and punches the number for Penthouse A. "Hello, Mr. Ford," she says, smiling into the phone. "Nope, sorry. Danica again. Abby asked me to tell you she'd prefer not to speak to you and that she's not coming up to your room because you treated her like a piece of shit and that's simply not acceptable." She winks at me, and then listens to whatever he's saying. Her eyes go wide with obvious shock. "Okay, hang on." She puts the call on hold. "Lucas Ford said to tell you, 'I'm sorry, Abby. Please forgive me. I was an asshole and I deserved everything you said, and more, and I'll never do it again. Now will you *please* get your stubborn ass up to my room so I can show you that I am, in fact, capable of treating you like a human being?'" Danica puts her hands on her hips. "What the *fuck* is going on, Abby?"

I ignore Danica's question, and instead lean forward and whisper, "Tell that bastard if he's truly sorry he can get his VIP rock star ass down here and apologize to my face like a gentleman, or else he can go to motherfucking hell."

Danica gasps in shock. "*Abby.*"

I continue. "And if you don't say all that to him, word for word, I swear I'll never forgive you as long as I live."

Danica looks like she's going to have a stroke. Of course, she knows my threat is absolutely ridiculous. I love her to pieces and she knows it and nothing will ever change that, but she's never witnessed even a distant glimmer of this side of my personality before, and clearly she didn't even suspect it existed. "Who *are* you?" she whispers as she picks up the phone, but she's smiling devilishly from ear to ear as she says it. "Hi, Mr. Ford," she says primly into the telephone. "Nope. Danica again. Yes, sir, I told Abby your message exactly as you conveyed it to me, but she's still refusing to come up to your room. Actually, she has a message for you which I'm now going to deliver to you word for word, so please don't shoot the messenger, okay?" She clears her throat. "Abby told me to tell you, '*If you're truly sorry, you can get your VIP rock star ass down here and apologize to my face like a gentleman, or else you can go to motherfucking hell.*'"

My heart is beating wildly. I just went all-in and I know it. If Lucas doesn't take the bait, I'll have no more chips to play and this delicious game will be over.

Time stops as Danica listens to whatever Lucas is saying.

I can't stand it. My heart is hammering like a steel drum with anticipation.

Finally, Danica says brightly, "I'll tell her, Mr. Ford. Thank you." She gently places the phone receiver in its cradle and grins at me. "Mr. Ford said, 'Goddamnit!'" She giggles. "And *then* he said, 'Fine. Tell that ass-kicker I'll be right down.'"

CHAPTER NINE

I'm holding my breath as I stare at the elevator bank in anticipation of Lucas Ford emerging to apologize for his boorish behavior. I can't help worrying this might be some sort of trick. Is he coming down here to embarrass me again the same way he did the other night in his suite, but this time in front of Danica? Or will he apologize to me sincerely?

Loud singing and giggling erupts to my right, and when I look toward the noise I see a gaggle of thirty-something-year-old women entering the lobby, fresh from what looks like a drunken night out. A girls' trip or bachelorette party, I presume. We get that sort of thing a lot here at The Rockford.

I make my way from behind the front desk toward the loud revelers, my fake smile firmly in place. "Hey, ladies," I say. "I'm sorry to be a buzzkill, but you're going to have to take the volume down a bit so we don't—"

"*Oh my God,*" one of the women blurts, her eyes fixed on a target behind me.

"Lucas Ford!" another one yells.

"I love you!" a third woman shrieks.

And they're off, rushing past me in a frenzy of excitement.

I whirl around to find Lucas standing fifteen feet away in a dark gray T-shirt and jeans, half-heartedly waving at the women as they rush him. And in seconds—whether he's in the mood to be ambushed or not—he's sucked into the eye of a tornado. Wow, these women are relentless. They're taking selfies, giving Lucas hugs and kisses, and enthusiastically fawning all over him. One of the women rummages into her purse for a pen and asks Lucas to sign her boob—which he does, much to the shrieking delight of the group. Another member of the group calls her sister, who apparently was dead asleep when the call came in, and shoves her phone under Lucas's nose and demands he sing happy birthday to her.

I amble behind the front desk, watching the frenzy. "Wow," I whisper to Danica. "Dance, monkey boy, dance."

"Give the poor dude some personal space," Danica whispers back.

"If this is Lucas's daily life," I whisper, "I wouldn't switch places with him for anything."

Finally, after Lucas has kissed every last one of his adoring fans and sung to the sister and signed the boob and posed for selfies and signed a cell phone cover and grocery receipt and chuckled and smiled and been as gracious as any rock star could possibly be, he waves to the women and says, "Okay, I've got to do my thing now, ladies. Have a great night."

The women titter and giggle and hug him and kiss him again, and finally head toward the elevators on a cloud of euphoria, finally leaving Lucas free to approach the front desk.

"Hello, Mr. Ford. *Sir*," I say, punctuating that last word with unmistakable snark.

"Hey, Abby the *Assassin*," he replies. He rests his muscled forearms on the counter between us. "I've decided Ass-kicker doesn't do you justice anymore." He rolls his eyes and it takes all my willpower not to grin. "Can I talk to you privately for a sec?" he asks. He motions toward a quiet corner of the lobby. "Please?"

"Whatever you have to say to me, you can say it in front of Danica," I say primly. I cross my arms over my chest.

Lucas cocks his head to the side and flashes me a panty-melting smile I've not seen from him before. A smile that plainly tells me he finds my attitude toward him highly amusing.

"What is it, Mr. Ford?" I ask. "I'm listening."

Lucas looks at Danica. "Can you give us a minute?"

"*Stay*," I command to Danica, not taking my eyes off Lucas.

Danica fidgets but doesn't leave.

Lucas exhales with obvious exasperation.

"Say what you need to say here, Mr. Ford. And please get to it. I've got some reports to do."

"*Abby*," Danica chastises me.

But I don't care if I'm being bad. This asshole deserves everything I'm serving up to him and more. I continue staring at Mr. Rock Star, my jaw clenched, waiting to find out if this is a trick or the real deal.

"Jesus," he finally mutters, shaking his head. He runs his hand through his hair and exhales. "I'm sorry I was a dick to you, Abby. Please forgive me. Sometimes, I forget the world doesn't revolve around me. Because, you know, the world actually does revolve around me." He smirks. "Now, would you *please* come to my suite so I can show you something?"

"Whatever you want to show me, I've already seen it," I say.

"I've seen your sex tape, remember?"

Danica snickers.

But Lucas doesn't seem to find my comment funny. In fact, he looks like he wants to strangle me. I must admit, it's a good look for him. "I don't want to show you my dick," he says, his jaw clenched. "If that's what I want, I could have fucked the woman who asked me to sign her tit and tried to slip me her room key." He rolls his eyes. "Abby, I want to play you a song I wrote. A song about *you.*"

My jaw drops.

Lucas flashes me a cocky smile. "And *then* I want to show you my dick." He grins at Danica and she literally snorts. Lucas looks at me again. "So will you *please* come up to my suite now? I'm not going to stand here begging you all night. People are gonna come in and swarm me again if I stand here much longer and I'm not in the mood to be Lucas Fucking Ford tonight. I'm tired—really fucking tired, Abby—and in the middle of an amazing writing session. So, decide. Are you coming with me or not? You've got three seconds to make your decision and then I'm out."

I look at Danica, my brain short-circuiting and my heart racing.

"Three... two..." Lucas says.

"Oh, for fuck's sake," Danica blurts. "*Go,* Abby! He's Lucas Fucking Ford!"

CHAPTER TEN

Lucas presses the button for Penthouse A while I stand as far away from him inside the elevator as possible. I'm pretty much crapping my pants. Lucas Ford wrote a song about me? And now he's going to play it for me privately...in his suite? My fifteen-year-old self would need the crash cart.

"I really am sorry I was such an asshole to you," Lucas mumbles. "It had nothing to do with you. I'd had a particularly rough show that night and I guess I took it out on you. Sorry."

I nod, acknowledging his apology. "We all have bad nights. Nobody's perfect, not even rock stars."

"Especially not rock stars."

"Yeah, well, hotel clerks aren't perfect either, so don't feel too bad."

"What?" Lucas says, feigning shock. "Miss Indoor Clean Air Act of 2007 isn't perfect?"

"2006. And no, I'm not. I'm actually more fucked up than you could possibly imagine."

The elevator doors open and Lucas politely motions for me to step outside first, which I do, and then we walk down the short hall toward Penthouse A.

"You couldn't possibly be more fucked up than me," Lucas says as we walk. "I signed a four-record deal with my label at seventeen. A deal that gave those cocksuckers full creative control." He sighs. "I've just got to get them to green-light the songs for my fourth and final album and I'll finally be free." He sighs. "Unfortunately, that's a whole lot easier said than done."

"That doesn't sound like you're 'fucked up,'" I say. "It just sounds like you're creatively fucked."

"Same thing. If I'm not the master of my own creative destiny, there's no point to any of it. Trust me, being creatively fucked has led to me being royally *fucked up*."

We reach the door to the penthouse and Lucas opens the door for me, and the moment we're inside, he strides to the couch and grabs his acoustic guitar. "Have a seat, Assassin," he says, indicating a chair a few feet away.

I sit and immediately notice two sets of sandwiches and side dishes on the coffee table.

Lucas begins tuning his guitar. "I assume you like BLTs? That's what you ordered the other night."

I feel my cheeks coloring. "They're my favorite. Thank you. That was thoughtful of you."

"It's the least I can do. Or, hey, that's what this cute little ass-kicker assassin told me is the least I can do. And thank God for that. When you left the other night after spectacularly kicking my ass, this song flowed out of me like lava from a volcano. It was like it was already written in some secret code and I just needed to unlock it." His eyes are on fire. "Man, it felt incredible to have a song pour out of me like that again. It's been a really long time."

My heart is racing. "I'm elated for you."

"I've had pretty severe writer's block for about three years," he says. "I haven't been able to write a damned thing. At least not for myself. I've written a ton of junk-pop bullshit for plenty of other artists. Tons and tons, actually. But no 'Lucas Ford' songs. After a while, it seemed pointless to try. My label owns my soul and they kept vetoing the songs I sent them. Why bother?"

"Don't they want to release the fourth and final album of your contract as much as you do?"

"Only if it's filled with the kind of songs *they* want me to release. Only if I'm 'on brand.'" He shakes his head with disgust. "And if not, that's fine with them. I can stay in artistic purgatory forever as far as they're concerned. Honestly, I think it gives 'em a raging boner to keep me locked in the tower."

"But that's against their own economic interest."

"Welcome to the music industry, sweetheart." He begins strumming his guitar as he speaks. "I've been a pretty big dick to those cocksuckers for the past five years, so it's become personal. They've deserved my wrath, no doubt, but it's only recently dawned on me it doesn't matter if they deserve it. Being an asshole to them is ultimately the same thing as being an asshole to myself. At this point, I've decided to grow up once and for all and do whatever I've got to do to get out from under this fucking contract, even if that means writing whatever 'Lucas Ford' songs I'm contractually obligated to write. But that's easier said than done. Creativity doesn't work on command. I mean, you know, writing bullshit songs for another artist? Pfft. Like falling off a log. But writing songs that resonate emotionally? The kind those cocksuckers will approve for a Lucas Ford album? Yeah, that's really fucking hard." He flashes me a huge smile. "Until the other night, that is. Right after I met you." His smile broadens. "Abby the Ass-kicker kicked my ass without holding back and *bam*! The most badass song in the history of the universe popped out like I'd ordered it from a vending machine." He laughs. "It was the damnedest thing ever." His strumming of his guitar has become more and more energized. "Okay, enough talking, Assassin. You ready to hear my song?"

I nod, every molecule in my body feeling like it's buzzing.

"Okay, here it is. It's called... You guessed it... 'Assassin.'"

Without further ado, Lucas launches into an upbeat, catchy song about "a girl who looks like a slice of the sun" but who, it turns out, "is an assassin, son. She makes her way as a hired gun, taking shit as she goes from no one. Assassin kicks your ass so hard you cry, tells you the truth, makes you wish for the lie. When she's done with you, it's your turn to die. She's a killer, son, an assassin. Fall in love with this girl as she walks out the door. But she leaves you for dead, leaves you begging for more. She's a killer at large, a *femme fatale*. Don't fall in love with this one, she's an assassin."

Lucas's voice is oozing with sex appeal as he sings. His song's melody is instantly memorable and addictive, and his guitar playing is swoon worthy. In short, I'm in heaven. This is the Lucas Ford I've always adored. The sexy troubadour who burst onto the scene a decade ago with "Shattered Hearts" and stole the entire world's collective heart.

When Lucas is done performing his new song, he looks up from his guitar and beams a sexy smile at me, his eyes smoldering. "So what do you think, Assassin? You dig it?"

I clap and swoon. "I dig it," I say, feeling light-headed. "It's amazing." I clutch my racing heart. "I think this is one of the most exciting moments of my life. Gimme a minute. I seriously can't breathe."

Lucas chuckles and puts down his guitar. "I'm glad you like it."

"No, no, I *love* it. It's going to be a smash hit. I'm positive your label's going to approve it for your album."

"Yeah, they already did. I recorded a quick demo of it on my iPad and sent it to the warden earlier. He and the rest of the cocksuckers went apeshit over it. Finally, after four fucking years, we've got a mutually agreed upon first song for my final album. Hallelujah."

"Wow, congratulations."

Lucas's eyes are positively sparkling. "Thanks to you. I couldn't have written it without you."

"Me? I didn't do anything except call you an asshole."

Lucas grins. "You did quite a bit more than that. You spoke the truth, which allowed me to peek inside your soul. Just for a split second there, but it was enough. Exactly what I needed, as it turned out." His eyes are burning with sexual heat. "*You inspired me, Abby.*"

Arousal whooshes between my legs. "Oh...well...whatever I did, I'm glad it helped you. Anytime."

Lucas shoots me a wicked smile. "I was hoping you'd say that."

My clit is pulsing, just that fast. Something really dirty just flashed across Lucas's mind. I could see it in his eyes.

"You hungry, Assassin?" he asks.

I look at him sideways, trying to decipher the expression on his face. "Um, sure," I reply. "Thanks."

Lucas hands me a full plate from the coffee table and we both begin tearing into the food he's ordered for us.

"So where are you from, Abby?" he asks politely. But before I can answer, he batters me with more questions. "Tell me a bit about yourself, Abby. What are your goals and ambitions, Abby? *What's your favorite color, Abby*?"

I return his snarky expression with one of my own. "You've got a good memory."

"Just making sure I don't get my ass kicked again by a certain assassin."

We share a smile.

"Seriously. Tell me a bit about yourself," he says. "You're an enigma to me. I can't quite figure you out."

"That makes two of us," I say. "I can't quite figure me out, either."

Lucas chuckles. "It's now abundantly clear to me you're not at all what you seem."

"You said that before."

"But this time I mean it in a whole new way. Now I can physically *smell* it on you."

I'm mortified. "You can smell *what* on me?"

He closes his eyes and inhales deeply. "Your aroma. Your body's unique perfume." He opens his eyes and stares me down. "It gives you away."

I look at him like he's crazy.

"You know what I'd call your aroma if I were going to bottle it and sell it as a perfume?" he asks, his eyes positively smoldering.

"What?" I manage to ask.

"'Secretly Dirty.'"

My clit flutters. I hold his gaze. "Good name."

Lucas smirks. "So tell me about yourself, Abby. Let's talk like actual human beings...for a bit."

Oh, Jesus. I know where this is headed. He's following the exact blueprint I gave him, after all. And I must admit, I'm not sad about it.

I stammer through some boring basics about myself and he listens intently like what I'm telling him is endlessly fascinating.

"And what do you do for fun, Abby Medford?" he asks.

"I don't have time for fun, Lucas Ford."

"No?"

"No."

"I don't believe it."

"Believe it."

"Bullshit." He squints at me. "What'd you do last night when you had the night off?"

"I went on a date with this guy from school."

"Well, that sounds *fun*."

I shrug.

"Was the guy good in bed?"

"I didn't sleep with him."

"No?"

"No. He bored me to death so I cut our date short, right in the middle of making out with him. I wasn't trying to be a tease. I was genuinely testing the waters to see if I could force myself to feel attraction to a guy like him, but I couldn't."

"A guy like him?"

Our eyes are locked. My heart is pounding in my ears. "A nice guy."

"You don't like nice guys." It's a statement, not a question.

I nod. "I'm trying to change that about myself. I know I *should*.

MISADVENTURES ON THE NIGHT SHIFT

But it's easier said than done."

Lucas purses his beautiful lips. "What'd you do after you left Mr. Nice Guy last night?"

"I went back to my apartment."

"And?"

"And I put on 'Shattered Hearts' at full volume on my headphones so I wouldn't hear the loud buzzing sound of my vibrator."

His eyes ignite. "And?"

"And I watched your sex tape and used my vibrator and listened to your voice. And within thirty seconds I made myself come so freaking hard I left a puddle on my sheets."

Unmistakable sexual desire washes over his features. His guitar is covering his crotch, but by the look on his face I'd bet any amount of money he's hard as a rock right now.

"Did you watch the edited or unedited version of my sex tape?" he asks.

"Edited. I tried to watch the unedited version, but it had been taken down everywhere I searched for it."

"Ah. My trusty lawyers, hard at work."

"I thought you said the blonde leaked the video with your permission."

"She did. But it wouldn't have done her any good if the whole world thought I didn't give a shit about it, now would it? For her to get the most mileage out of the video, it had to be 'the sex tape Lucas Ford doesn't want anyone to see.'" He shrugs. "We've all got our parts to play."

"What mileage is she trying to get?"

"She's got a hard-on to star in a reality TV show, so I said I'd help her as a favor."

"Who is she?"

"My best friend's girlfriend."

"You had sex with your best friend's *girlfriend*?"

"As a favor, like I said. She and my friend figured a leaked sex tape with Lucas Ford was the quickest way to get her a show." He reaches for a box of cigarettes. "It was just sex. No biggie. My buddy would have done the same for me, I'm sure. And it certainly wasn't traumatizing to me, as I'm sure you observed."

I've been rendered speechless.

He puts a cigarette between his lips and lights it. "So do you have any 'fangirl' questions for me, Abby? You mentioned you might have a couple the other night. Lemme guess, you want to know the story behind 'Shattered Hearts'?"

"Yeah, actually. I get the feeling there's more to the lyrics than what's on the surface."

He takes a long drag off his cigarette and studies me. "I never tell anyone the full story behind that song. I tell a modified version. Boy meets girl, boy loses girl, boy never gets girl back and he's brokenhearted." He takes another hit off his cigarette. "But you know what? Just because you were so damned honest with me the other night when you ripped me a new asshole, I'm going to tell you the whole truth in return."

My heart leaps.

"Hang on. I got to get comfortable for this conversation." He carefully sets his guitar down next to him and strips off his T-shirt, making my jaw hang open.

"I hate clothes," he says by way of explanation. "Okay, so 'Shattered Hearts.'" He takes a deep drag off his cigarette. "Do you remember my original drummer from my first album? Cole Larchmont?"

"No, I, uh..." I fight staring at his abs. *I want to lick them.* "When I, uh, went to your concert way back when, I don't think I noticed anyone or anything onstage but you."

He smiles. "Cole was my first drummer. He wound up quitting my band right after the first tour because he decided no amount of money could possibly be enough to make him want to be in the same room with me, let alone make music with me."

My stomach seizes.

"Cole and I had been best friends our whole lives. Grew up together. I'm an only child and he was the brother I never had. When we were seventeen, about six months before I got my record deal, Cole fell in love with this pretty, sassy, girl-next-door type named Winona. *Winnie.* You remind me of her, actually."

Goose bumps erupt on my skin. Did Lucas just indirectly call me pretty and sassy?

"Man, did Cole fall hard for Winnie," Lucas continues. "He wanted to marry her and take her on tour with us one day if we became big rock stars and maybe even have a little baby with her and a white picket fence. Damn, was Cole in love with that pretty, sassy girl."

There it is again! Lucas just indirectly called me pretty and sassy! I'm not making that up, am I?

"So, of course," Lucas continues, "since Cole was like a brother to me, that should have made Winnie like a sister to me, too, right?

But it didn't." He sucks on his cigarette. "Because, unfortunately, I was head over heels in love with Winnie, too."

My breathing hitches. *Ten seconds ago he said I remind him of Winnie!*

"No one knew how I felt about Winnie," he continues. "I acted like I didn't give a shit about her and said dicky things to her all the time and never said a word about her to Cole. In fact, once or twice, Cole begged me to be nicer to her." He looks at me pointedly. "I'm pretty sure his exact words were 'Come on, Luke, treat her like an actual human once in a while, would you?'"

My heart stops.

He smiles at whatever he's seeing on my face. "But I couldn't be sweet to her. I couldn't be anything but an asshole to her. *Because she owned me.* And I knew that wouldn't end well for me. But after a while I couldn't help myself. I was obsessed with her. Couldn't eat or sleep. Thought about her night and day. Dreamed about her. As far as I was concerned, she was perfect in every way."

I can't breathe. I can't think. I can't function. A moment ago he said I remind him of Winnie, didn't he? Was I imagining that?

"I thought about her when I fucked someone else," Lucas continues. "I jacked off to fantasies about her. I was tortured. And you know what tortured me the most? The way Cole and Winnie were always macking down on each other around me. Like I wasn't even there. They couldn't keep their hands off each other. So, of course, that just made me want her more. *It made me covet her.* But I stayed strong. I knew Cole would never forgive me if I laid a pinkie on his beloved Winnie, so I stayed away from her and treated her like shit as best I could to make her hate me... All the while fucking any girl who even remotely reminded me of her. And then..." He exhales a long, dejected breath. "One day, I lost my willpower. Cole was off doing something one night and Winnie and I were alone, watching a movie or whatever, and I just stopped giving a shit about consequences. I wanted her. Nothing could stop me. Not even my loyalty to Cole." He shakes his head mournfully. "So I made my move and Winnie and I wound up fucking like animals. It was unbelievable. Like, the world shook for me, you know? So we became addicted to each other and started fucking around behind Cole's back every chance we got. Chickenshit thing to do, I know, but neither of us wanted to hurt him, and we thought we could get it out of our systems and then everything would return to normal. Honestly, we both really did love Cole and thought for sure a nice girl like Winnie was supposed to wind up with a nice guy like Cole, not an asshole like me." He looks wistful for a long moment. "Well, needless to say, the story didn't end the way we thought it would. In fact, it ended with three shattered hearts."

I stare at him for a long moment. He's stunning right now. Absolutely breathtaking. Truly, the most beautiful man I've ever beheld. "Do you still love her?" I ask softly.

"I don't know if I ever did," he says, surprising me. "I've thought about it a lot and I think it's fifty-fifty I just wanted what I couldn't have. Maybe my stupid seventeen-year-old brain confused envy for love? I dunno."

"But you said the earth shook when you had sex with her," I say.

"Oh, it did." He sighs. "Shit, maybe I did love her. I sure thought so at the time. Maybe nowadays my memories of the way I felt are tainted by how much pain my actions wound up causing. Winnie didn't start something with me. I made a move on *her*. I'm positive she never would have betrayed Cole if it weren't for me."

"Winnie was just as culpable as you were. It takes two to tango."

Lucas shakes his head and stubs out his cigarette hastily. "Fuck, I don't know. I'm the last guy to ask about love these days. You've got to be an actual human to feel love, right? And I haven't been human for a good four or five years. I'm nothing but a dancing monkey."

"Lucas," I whisper, my heart panging for him.

Lucas slaps his hands on his thighs, signaling the emphatic end of this particular topic of conversation. "So you got anymore fangirl questions burning a hole in your pocket, Ass-kicker?"

I shake my head.

"Cool. So now I've got a question for you. Would you be willing to do me a huge favor?"

"Anything."

"Would you watch my sex tape while I watch you? Ever since you told me you touched yourself after watching it and made yourself come, I haven't been able to stop fantasizing about watching you do exactly that."

I'm shocked and I'm sure my face shows it. I glance down at his crotch. He's most definitely sporting wood behind his jeans. My face feels hot. I open my mouth and abruptly shut it.

Lucas shifts his position on the couch, obviously relieving pressure on his hard-on. "I want to show you the *unedited* version. The one where I come all over her tits." He takes a deep, steadying breath. "I want to watch you touch yourself. I want to see your facial expressions as you watch me fuck her. I want to hear the noises you make as you get yourself off. And then I want to see you come so hard you wet my fucking sheets."

CHAPTER ELEVEN

I lie on my back on Lucas's fluffy white bed, fully clothed, my heart racing, awaiting instruction on how Mr. Rock Star wants this pervy party to go down. "Like this?" I ask.

"Perfect." Lucas pulls a laptop out of his bag and sets it next to me on the bed. "I'm gonna sit over there." He points to an armchair in the corner. "Okay with you?"

"Okay," I breathe, ogling his beautiful, shirtless torso.

He opens a video file on his computer and leaves it paused on the screen. "Start it up when I say," he says, settling into his chair in the corner. "I want you to pretend you're alone in your bedroom. You have no idea I'm sitting here watching you."

I can't believe I'm doing this. I've never masturbated in front of someone before. And now I'm going to do it for the first time for Lucas Ford? "Do you want me to undress?" I ask.

"No. I want you to touch yourself underneath your skirt and slide your fingers inside your undies. I want to wish I could see your pussy, but I can't."

Oh, Jesus, the bulge in his jeans is doing wonders to heighten my arousal. "Okay," I whisper.

"Would you be comfortable with me jerking myself off while I watch?"

I nod. "It would turn me on."

"Good." He unbuttons his jeans but doesn't pull out his dick. "Start the video, Abby."

I take a deep breath and press play on the video and there he is onscreen. The one and only Lucas Ford. Naked, tattooed, and fully erect. Preening like a peacock. I focus on the real article in the corner and my brain instantly connects the dots between the naked dude with the massive hard-on I'm viewing on the laptop and the guy with the huge bulge behind his jeans in the corner.

"Don't look at me," Lucas whispers from the corner. "I'm peeking through your window."

Holy shit. I shift my eyes back to the computer screen and slide my fingers underneath my skirt, into my panties, and straight into my warm wetness. "I'm already super wet," I whisper.

Lucas lets out an audible breath in the corner.

Naked Lucas in the video has stopped preening and now he's sliding his hand between the blonde's legs. Fingering her. Hulking over her from behind. She cries out with pleasure. He grips her hair and buries his massive dick inside her.

Oh, yeah, my fingers are finding their rhythm now. I'm so damned wet, my body's making a kind of sloshing sound as my fingers work their magic. "I'm so turned on," I murmur softly.

I hear Lucas moan in the corner and can't resist peeking over at him, despite his strict instructions to the contrary. He's got his dick and balls pulled out of his unbuttoned jeans and he's pumping his shaft with fervor, his face intense.

I shift my eyes back to the computer screen and the movement of my fingers intensifies.

Naked Lucas on the computer is now fucking the blonde with deep, ferocious thrusts while fondling her large breast with his free hand. I peek at the live version of Lucas in the corner again. Wow, he's going to town on himself.

Lucas's burning eyes in the corner lock with mine. He looks on the cusp of orgasm to me.

And I'm right there with him.

"Oh, God," I moan, and Lucas's face contorts with pleasure at the sound of my obvious arousal.

My eyes flicker to the computer screen again. And then back to Lucas pumping his shaft in the corner. I notice the sexy bead of wetness pooling at the tip of Lucas's penis. I gaze at his balls. His abs. His blazing dark eyes and tousled hair. I'm going to lose it any second. My toes curl. I hold my breath.

"Oh, fuck," Lucas blurts on the video.

"Watch the video," Lucas commands from his chair in the corner. "I want to see your face when I come all over her tits."

I return to the laptop as instructed, just in time to see Lucas push the blonde onto the bed, grab his dick, and shoot his milky-white load all over her massive breasts.

And...I'm gone. Every muscle connected to my clit seizes violently and then begins clenching and unclenching in warm, delicious waves. I spread my legs and arch my back, reveling in my delectable climax.

"Oh, fuck," Lucas blurts in the corner, and a half second later he stiffens, leans back in his chair, and shoots a large load all over his bare, taut abs, emitting a long guttural groan as he does.

There's stillness.

Finally, Lucas exhales a long sigh of deep satisfaction.

But I'm not satisfied. Not even close. In fact, my body feels like it's just getting started.

Lucas exhales loudly from his seat in the corner and runs his hand through his tousled hair. "Holy fuck, you're hot."

But I'm not in the mood to talk. I'm in the mood to taste him. To ingest him. *To conquer him.*

Without consciously commanding my body to do it, I get up from the bed and walk toward him, sucking my wet fingers as I go. I kneel before him and voraciously lap up every drop of goodness off his abs like a stray kitten lapping milk from a saucer.

"Lucas," I whisper, my fingers between my legs, my body aching painfully for him. "I want you so fucking bad."

CHAPTER TWELVE

When I've licked every drop of goodness off Lucas's stomach, he grabs my hair and guides my face to within an inch of his. But before my lips meet their target, Lucas stops and holds me firm, his chest heaving, our eyes locked.

"Assassin," he whispers, his eyes burning.

I'm panting. Wet and swollen. *Aching.* Now that the drug of him has infiltrated my blood stream, I want more. *I want all of him.*

His hand still buried in my hair, Lucas beams an amused smile at me that tells me he can see right through me. *He knows what I am.*

Lucas stands, guiding me up by my hair as he goes. When we're both standing, our bodies mere inches apart, he grips my hair extra hard and leans forward. I close my eyes, anticipating the thrill of finally getting to feel his luscious lips on mine, but much to my disappointment, he doesn't kiss me. He releases his brutal grip on me and begins stroking my hair from root to end. "I've got a proposition for you, dirty girl," he whispers, still stroking my hair. "Something I want you to do for me."

I open my eyes, quivering with desire, the taste of him still on my tongue. Whatever self-respect I managed to tap into the other night when I told him off for acting like an asshole is long gone now. I want him however I can get him. Even if I have to grovel.

Lucas smiles like he's deeply amused by something he sees in my face. "Come have a drink with me in the other room and I'll explain what I want from you." He releases me and motions politely toward the living room as if he's just asked me to join him for a spot of tea and crumpets.

I take a deep breath and walk on wobbly legs into the sitting area, my entire body trembling.

"Have a seat," he says, heading toward the bar on the other side of the room.

I sit on the couch.

"Beer? Whiskey?" he asks.

I bite my lip. Drinking alcohol on the job is a terminable offense. But hey, I've got to assume licking a guest's semen off his abs is equally prohibited. "Whiskey," I reply.

"A girl after my own heart." He pours two whiskeys, hands me one, and settles himself onto the opposite end of the couch. Too far away for our legs to touch, I notice.

I take a long sip of my drink, shuddering as the burning liquid goes down. "So what's your proposition?" I ask. "You've got my undivided attention."

"And you've got mine," he replies.

I bite my lip.

Lucas sips his whiskey, staring me down with burning eyes. "I want you to be my muse this week."

"Your *muse*?" I ask.

He nods.

"Sorry, I don't understand."

Lucas smiles. "Maybe I should give you a little background

information." He sips his whiskey again, apparently gathering his thoughts. "As I mentioned," he says, "my label owns me for four albums, thanks to the shitty-ass deal I signed as a puppy, and I've still got one more album to go before I'm free to do whatever the fuck I want. Unfortunately, my label and I have been fighting for quite some time about the direction of my last album and it's now clear to me there's only one way out of my indentured servitude. I've got to write an album's worth of songs the cocksuckers will approve, including the one song they're demanding above all others. A certain leadoff single they're forcing me to write. If I don't give 'em that one particular song, they've said they're fully prepared to hold the entire album hostage for however long it takes, no matter what other awesome songs I might write for it."

"What's the leadoff single they want?" I ask.

"Another 'Shattered Hearts.' Something that hits all the same emotional themes and chords."

I furrow my brow. "But that song was one of a kind. That's why everyone loves it so much."

"Try telling that to the cocksuckers. They're not songwriters. They're bean counters. And greedy bastards. And that's what they say I need to give them to release my fourth album and set me free from my contractual obligations."

"But what about 'Assassin'?" I ask. "Can't that one be the leadoff single? It's amazing."

"Yeah, it's a great song, for sure, and it'll definitely go on the album. The cocksuckers already approved it, thank God. But no matter how great 'Assassin' is, it's not the leadoff single they want. They want another 'Shattered Hearts' and nothing else will do." His eyes blaze with barely contained fury. "What they don't get is that I'm not being a dick about not writing a song like that. I literally *can't do it*. How could I? A guy's got to be able to *feel* something to write a brutal song like that, and I haven't felt an actual emotion in five fucking years." His eyes light up. "That is, until a certain ass-kicker chewed me out, and I discovered I just might have a few embers burning deep inside me, after all."

"But all I did was tell you to go fuck yourself. Obviously, 'Assassin' was inside you all along, just waiting to pop out."

"Yeah, it was there, for sure. But I couldn't *access* it. I couldn't *feel* it until you came along and lit my fuse. Abby, I haven't felt creatively inspired like that in years, and now that I've remembered what it feels like, I feel addicted. I want more."

My mind is reeling. "But what exactly are you asking me to do this week? Fuck you...or call you an asshole and stomp out?"

Lucas smiles like a shark. "All of the above."

I make a face that tells him I'm completely lost.

Lucas sighs. "I want to do an extended role-play with you, Abby. I want to recreate what happened between Cole, Winnie, and me ten years ago. But on a vastly condensed timeline and all of it right here in this suite."

I stare at him blankly, still not understanding.

"We're going to role-play having an illicit love affair behind my best friend's back," Lucas explains. "And then, at the end of our love affair, you're gonna break my heart."

My mind is racing. "You're asking me to role-play...being Winnie?"

"No. We'll be ourselves, but in an agreed-upon make-believe

scenario. I truly believe if we act out the scenario I have in mind, and we don't break character the whole time and really immerse ourselves in the fantasy, I'll start to feel all the right emotions—albeit in simulation—and ultimately feel inspired to write the required song. I mean, shit, I wrote 'Assassin' about you without knowing or loving you and anyone hearing it would swear I wrote it for a girl I'm head over heels in love with. So I figure, 'Why not use the same strategy to write 'Shattered Hearts' two point oh?'"

"But here's what I don't understand," I say. "If I'm your 'Winnie,' and you're our Lucas, then who'd be our 'Cole'?"

Lucas grins. "My best friend, Camden. My drummer since Cole left the band."

My stomach seizes. "So Camden and I would...?"

"You and Camden would role-play being in love, exactly the way Cole and Winnie were, and I'd watch and secretly *covet* you."

I swallow hard, suddenly quite certain where this thing is headed. "You're asking me to make out with Camden in front of you?"

"Not quite. I'm not seventeen anymore. I'm a grown-ass man who's been around the block a time or two. I don't think you and Camden getting handsy and kissing in front of me will get me where I need to go." He smiles wickedly. "So I'm asking you to fuck Camden. And to let me watch."

My mouth hangs open. *Oh my God.*

Lucas takes a languid sip of his whiskey, his eyes smoldering. "I'll watch and covet and ultimately break down and claim you for myself behind Camden's back. And after a few days of us covertly getting together, you'll shatter my heart by telling me you've realized you don't love me after all."

To my shame, warmth oozes between my legs at the very idea of what he's suggesting. Holy hell, this is depraved. And hot as hell. "This is crazy," I say, despite the excitement coursing through my veins. "What normal woman would say yes to this?"

"A normal woman probably wouldn't say yes," Lucas concedes. "But you're not a normal woman, are you, Assassin? In fact, I'd bet just about anything my proposition is turning you on like crazy right now."

I stare at him for a long beat, my crotch swelling with blood. How the hell does he know that about me? "But," I sputter, "I've never even met Camden. I can't possibly agree to have sex with some random guy."

Lucas cocks his head slightly, his eyes burning. "Let's cut the bullshit, Abby. I've got to be at a show in LA in six days and I've agreed to write this damned song before I leave. We both know this idea is making you wet. I can see it all over your pretty little face. And even more than that, I can *smell* it on you. I bet if I reached into your panties right now my fingers would come out soaking wet."

I press my lips together. He's right, of course. I'm soaking wet. But still, I'm not sure I'm ready to say yes to this extended role-play idea of his, no matter how hot it makes me. Sure, it sounds like kinky fun, but what would be the consequences for me when it's over? I've worked hard to avoid triggers and keep myself on track these past five years. Will letting myself run amok in the way Lucas is suggesting lead to me falling off the wagon completely when the fantasy is over? Or will I be able to revert to my well-ordered, disciplined life again like nothing ever happened?

"Don't worry, Camden is fuckable," Lucas says, obviously misreading the source of my apprehension. "If I swung that way, I'd fuck him myself." He grabs his phone off the coffee table and swipes briefly. "See for yourself. Camden Donnelly."

I take the phone from Lucas and watch a short video of Camden playing drums, and quickly surmise he's right. Yes, Camden is highly fuckable. He's in his late twenties or early thirties, I'd guess, with strawberry-blond hair, facial hair, lean muscles, and tattoos. And man, can that dude play the drums like a freaking badass. Yeah, based on this video, it seems sex with Camden would turn out to be an extremely pleasurable physical experience, indeed. I hand Lucas back his phone, my crotch pulsing. "Camden's fuckable," I agree. "But even if I were to say yes to this exercise in depravity, why on earth would Camden say yes to it?"

"Well, first off, I'm not asking Camden to paint my house. I'm asking him to have sex with a pretty girl. Not a hardship."

My heart skips a beat at Lucas's use of the word "pretty" to describe me.

"But on top of that," Lucas continues, "Cam's got a vested interest in freeing me from my label. He knows the first thing I'm gonna do when I'm free is release an album with my band, not as 'Lucas Ford.' Cam's already written a couple of badass songs for the album. Plus, regardless of his self-interest, I'm sure Camden would do it simply as my friend, especially after what I did for his girlfriend."

My skin pricks. Is he implying...?

"Yeah," Lucas says, nodding. "Cam's girlfriend is the blonde I fucked in the sex tape."

I bolt up from the couch, suddenly too shocked to sit. "Camden's got a *girlfriend*?"

"Abby, sit down," Lucas says breezily. "False outrage isn't a good look on you, babe. We both know you're gonna do this. I'm getting really tired of the song and dance."

I sit. "I'm not faking outrage here. I'm genuinely shocked you're asking me to screw another man at all, let alone a guy with a girlfriend. Do you guys make a habit of swapping women?"

"No. This will be a first."

I rub my forehead. "Well, is Camden's girlfriend going to burst in here while he and I are in the middle of screwing and hurl a knife into my back?"

"Of course, not. Cam's girlfriend is the one who begged Camden to ask me to do the sex tape with her in the first place. *She begged him to ask me*." He scoffs. "Clearly, that woman's got an opportunistic attitude about monogamy. She'll be fine with this."

My mind is racing. This is crazy.

"Come on, Abby," Lucas says. "I promise you'll have fun. I'm told Camden's a real beast in the sack. Right before I fucked his girlfriend, she said to me, 'You better bring your A game, Luke. I'm spoiled these days by how well Cammy fucks me.' So it sounds like you're definitely in for a treat."

I feel like a deer in headlights. My brain knows I should be appalled by this indecent proposal, but my body can't seem to feel anything but exhilaration. If only I knew for sure this little game wouldn't cause my old tendencies to bubble up and consume me again, it'd be a no-brainer to say yes.

"Are you on the pill?" Lucas asks, drawing me out of my

thoughts.

"Huh?"

"Are you on the pill?"

"Uh. Yes."

"And you're clean?"

I nod. "I haven't had sex in quite some time and when I do, I use condoms."

"Cool. We'll use condoms, but still, it's good to know these things."

"You and Camden are both clean?"

Lucas nods. "Before I agreed to fuck his girlfriend for the world to see, Cam assured me they were both clean and exclusive—other than me fucking her, obviously—and I get checked regularly and always use condoms."

I scoff. "You don't 'always' use condoms. You didn't use one with the blonde."

"That was a special circumstance. We had to give everyone an extra-hot show." He shoots me a cocky grin. "But still, I was careful. Since I was riding bareback, I followed my rule and didn't come inside her."

"Your rule?"

"I don't come inside a woman without a condom. Ever. No exceptions."

"What if you're in a committed relationship and she's on the pill?"

"Well, first off, I'm never in a 'committed relationship.' And, regardless, even if I were convinced I was deeply in love with the best girl ever, she could swear on her life she's on the pill, and I wouldn't believe her as far as I could throw her."

"Jeez. No wonder you don't have any committed relationships. It's hard to do if you're not capable of trust."

Lucas waves dismissively. "Try being me for ten years and see how many women you trust to have taken a little pill just because they said they did." He clenches his jaw. "Everyone wants a piece of me. It's just the way it is."

"Well, I don't."

Lucas scoffs. "Sure, you do. I'm the guy whose face used to hang on your bedroom wall when you were fifteen. Getting to fuck me is gonna be the fulfillment of your teenage fantasy." He shrugs. "People tell me all the time I'm their 'desert island' pick or whatever. Some sort of bucket-list item. I'm just saying I don't expect you to be any different than anyone else."

I stand. "You're wrong about me. Completely wrong. I want nothing. You're the one asking *me* to be your muse, not the other way around. So if you're going to ask me to do this thing for you and then hold it against me if I do it, then let's forget the whole thing."

Lucas's face lights up. "Now see? That's what I'm talking about! That's my little ass-kicking muse right there."

I cross my arms over my chest, not sure if he's making fun of me or not.

"Sit down and cool your jets, Assassin. You're getting worked up for no reason."

I sit back down, pressing my lips firmly together.

"I was simply trying to explain what ten years of being 'Lucas Ford' gets a guy, okay? I'm just saying complete trust is impossible for me to achieve, at least with women. They've always got some sort of ulterior motive when it comes to me. Something they *want*. It's just the way it is and always will be."

"I refuse to believe every woman on planet Earth is looking to exploit you. If that's been your experience with women since you became famous, then you must not be looking in the right places for love."

Lucas shakes his head.

"Well, what about having a relationship with someone who's famous?" I ask. "Then you wouldn't be worried she's a gold digger or using you to get ahead."

Lucas swats at the air like I've said something patently ridiculous. "Actresses and singers are the worst. Famewhores like Camden's girl. All of 'em. Been there, done that. Plus, as a practical matter, being with someone else famous doubles the paparazzi waiting for me outside restaurants, and I fucking *hate* that shit."

"But I've seen countless photos of you with models and actresses over the years."

"Whatever you've seen is old. I haven't hooked up with someone like that in years, unless it was a one-night thing after a party or awards show, or a *fauxmance* set up by our publicists." He takes a long sip of his drink. "So what about you? How's the search for love for a civilian in the Age of Tinder?"

"The same as it is for you. I don't date celebrities because it doubles the paparazzi waiting for me outside restaurants."

He laughs.

"I'm not kidding," I say. "The minute I see paparazzi coming at me, I bolt in the other direction."

We share a smile.

"Seriously, though," he says. "How's the search for love and trust working out for a normal girl like you?"

"Not very well, honestly. About as well as it's going for you."

"Why? You're pretty, smart, semi-funny-ish. And you get angry in a flash, which is hella sexy. Just let your freak flag fly the way you've been doing with me and you'll have your pick of guys."

"Well, thanks for all those backhanded compliments. What girl doesn't want to be called semi-funny-ish? But, trust me, the way I'm behaving with you would be impossible to duplicate in the real world."

"Why?"

I shrug. "Just trust me. For reasons I don't care to talk about, this 'hella sexy' and 'semi-funny-ish' version of me you've got the good fortune of experiencing needs to stay firmly bottled up."

Lucas looks at me sideways, like he's trying to figure me out. "I've never met anyone quite like you before, Abby."

"That's so weird because I meet people like you every day of my life, Lucas Ford."

He laughs.

"So, come on, Rock Star," I say. "Let's figure out this Cole-Winnie-Lucas debacle, because I'm a working girl and I've got to get back to the front desk before I'm missed."

CHAPTER THIRTEEN

"So you'll do it?" Lucas asks.

"I didn't say that. I'm still deciding."

He sighs with exasperation. "What's left to decide? It's a no-brainer, Abby—a win-win-win. You get to have sex with your teenage fantasy. *You're welcome.* Camden gets to pay me back for helping his girl land a reality show, plus he gets to enjoy a fully sanctioned extracurricular fuck or two or three with a pretty, semi-funny-ish girl who—"

"Whoa, whoa, whoa. Camden gets to enjoy a fuck or two or *three*? How many times are you expecting me to have sex with your best friend before you deign to have sex with me yourself?"

"I don't know. I can't say with numerical certainty how many times it's gonna take 'til I'm so turned on I'm willing to stab my best friend in the back to have you."

I scoff. "So you're asking me to screw Camden all week long *hoping* you'll *maybe* get horny enough to want to have sex with me yourself?"

Lucas rolls his eyes like I've said something patently ridiculous. "Abby, of course I'm gonna fuck you—and sooner rather than later. I'm hard as a rock right now, dying to get inside you. All I'm saying is I don't want to preschedule the whole damned thing like we've got an itinerary. Like we're on a cruise ship and fucking each other is shuffleboard on the lido deck. That defeats the whole purpose."

"Which is what, again?"

"Me feeling the urge to steal you away *organically* so I feel seemingly real emotions when you ultimately kick me to the curb."

"This is a total mind-fuck, you know."

Lucas flashes me a wicked smile. "Awesome, huh?"

"That's not the word I'd use. If you're already hard and feeling attracted to me, then let's just have some awesome sex now. We'll start the role-play tomorrow. Let's seize the day."

"Nope. Torturing myself is what's going to make it so much sweeter when I finally break down."

"Lucas, for the love of fuck! I'm not going to have sex with Camden more than once, no matter what. I want *you*. That's the only reason I'm even thinking of doing this ridiculous thing."

Lucas smirks. "God, you're such a bullshitter. It's really quite amusing."

I glare at him.

"Just keep an open mind, okay? That's all I ask. If at any point you're not comfortable with what's happening, you'll say so and we'll stop. But going in, let's not say beforehand what we will or won't do. Let's let it unfold in the moment. If we stay in character and immerse ourselves in our roles completely, you might be surprised what turns you on."

I roll my eyes. "Okay, fine. I'll keep an open mind."

"Thank you."

"So walk me through what you envision happening after you've made your move on me, whenever that's going to be."

"Well, basically, I'll fall head over heels in love with you, and then you'll shatter my heart by telling me you don't love me, that you love Cole. And no matter how much I tell you I love you and want to be with you, or how many love songs I write you, nothing changes your mind. Your heart wants Cole and that's that. And then, at the end of all that, God willing, I'll sit down and write the second coming of 'Shattered Hearts' and finally be free to do whatever the fuck kind of music I want."

The tortured look on Lucas's face is killing me right now. "Camden," I say softly.

He looks at me quizzically.

"You said I'll tell you I still love '*Cole*.'"

Lucas smashes his lips together. "Oh. Yeah. Camden. Freudian slip." He looks wistful for a long moment, lost in a distant memory. "God, that sucked."

"I'm sorry she broke your heart, Lucas."

"I deserved it." He shrugs. "So let's talk about your fee, Assassin."

"My *fee*?"

"Correct."

"Lucas, you can't *pay* me to do this for you. I'm not a hooker. I'd be doing it because I want to help you."

"And because you're secretly a kinky little thing."

I smirk. "Yeah, that, too."

"Look, I get it, okay? But paying you is non-negotiable."

"I won't take your money."

"Abby, it's for your own good. Making this a business transaction will help you distinguish fantasy from reality when at the end of all this you've convinced yourself the emotions you're feeling for me are real and you don't want to break my heart after all."

I stare at him in disbelief. I can't believe my ears. He's fully expecting me to fall in love with him...*for real?*

"Think of yourself like an actor hired for a movie," Lucas continues. "Actors feel all kinds of emotions that seem real to them while they're filming. They cry, laugh, get turned on, whatever. That's why so many actors hook up with costars during a movie shoot and then quickly break up when it's over. They realize their emotions weren't real after all, even though it seemed like it at the time. If I pay you, your brain can explain the situation to your heart after the fact, and you'll have a much easier time moving on."

I'm flabbergasted. He's fully expecting me to fall head over heels in love with him *for real* at the end of this. And yet he's asking me to do it, anyway? That's just plain inhumane. I should walk out. I should tell him to forget it, that the stakes are too high for me, that I'm not the kind of girl who can come out of something like this unscathed.

But I don't say any of it.

Nope.

Because, whether I like it or not, he's reading me exactly right. I want him any way I can get him. Even if it's just for pretend, and no matter the risk to my fragile heart. I want him because he's Lucas Freaking Ford and I've loved him since I was fifteen. I want him because he's beautiful and a genius and the sexiest man alive. And, yes, I admit it. I want him, even like this, because I'm secretly a dirty little thing.

"So how much do you want?" Lucas asks. "Name your price."

"I don't want your money," I mutter.

"Duly noted, but payment is non-negotiable. I pay you or we

MISADVENTURES ON THE NIGHT SHIFT

don't do this. And we both know you want to do this as much as I do."

I bite the inside of my cheek for a while considering my reply. "Thirteen thousand, in cash," I finally say, expecting him to call me a greedy little bitch and cut the number in half.

But he doesn't.

"Done," he says. "A non-disclosure agreement will be waiting for you in an envelope at the front desk when you get into work tomorrow night. Bring the signed contract with you when you come up to the suite."

"I'd never tell anyone about this, whether I've been sworn to contractual secrecy or not."

"Then you should have no problem with signing my NDA." He waits for my response, his eyes trained on mine.

I sigh and nod.

"Good. I'll give you the first half of your fee tomorrow night and the second half toward the end of the week. I'll make the second half an incentive for you to follow through on your promise to crush my heart like a cockroach."

I don't reply. This is some fucked-up shit.

"So are you in or out, Ass-kicker? I need your final answer now. Time's up."

"Aren't you forgetting something? Even if I'm in, there's no guarantee Camden will be."

"Camden already said yes. I asked him before I called down to the lobby about your blazer. Oh, speaking of which, it's over there." He points to my blazer on the back of a nearby chair.

"How'd you explain this insanity to Camden?"

"I just told him the deal, straight up, and he laughed and said it sounded fun. He asked what you look like, so I sent him a little video I made of you when you were chewing me out at the door."

"What the hell?" I blurt. "You made a video of me? When?"

"When you turned toward the door midway through your rampage, I pressed record."

"Why?"

"Because you were turning me on. You were so damned *pissed* at me." He chuckles. "I was getting hard watching you yell at me and I figured you weren't done with me yet. So I thought, 'Hey, I might want to watch this little cutie kick my ass again later and jerk myself off.' So I pressed record."

Heat spreads throughout my body. "And did you...watch the video and jerk yourself off?"

"Yup. Twice. And I'm planning to do it a third time the minute you leave today."

My crotch is pulsing. "Lucas, this is crazy. Why jerk off to a video when you have the live version of me here with you now? You're turned on. I'm turned on. Forget about Camden. Forget the role-play. Let's have some fun. Touch between my legs and see for yourself how much I want you."

His eyes blaze. "Fuck, Abby. Don't do this to me. I want to fuck you right this very minute, I swear to God. But I can't do it. I can't lay a pinky on you."

"*Why?*"

"Because the game's already started. You're Camden's girl, not mine. And he's my best friend."

I throw up my hands. "Oh, for the love of fuck. This is insane."

"'There's a fine line between genius and insanity.'" He puts his empty glass down on the coffee table. "So what time are you coming tomorrow? Around the same time as tonight?"

I nod. "For the next two nights I can only come up during The Dead Zone, but the following two nights I'm off work, so I can stay as long as you please. I hope that's acceptable to you."

He flashes me a beaming smile. "Very acceptable. I'll plan to order some food tomorrow night so the three of us can eat and break the ice before you and Camden get down to bonin'."

"No, don't order any pre-bonin' food. I don't want to break the ice. Tell Camden the minute he opens the door, the role-play starts. He and I are in love and can't keep our hands off each other and you're his best friend with a secret woody for his best friend's girl. That way, there'll be no chance for me to get cold feet. Tell Camden he opens the door and the Hunger Games begin."

Lucas chuckles. "I'll let Cam know."

I get up from the couch, my head spinning. "All right. It's settled then. I'm officially a hooker."

"Yup. Practically a streetwalker."

I head toward the door and Lucas follows closely behind.

"Well, I guess I'll see you tomorrow, then," I say. "Tell Camden I look forward to...fucking him...for cash."

Lucas snickers. "I'll be sure to tell him." He opens the door of the suite and waves politely like I've just finished selling him solar panels. "'Bye, Assassin."

"'Bye, Pimp."

Lucas leans against the doorjamb as I walk past him, his bare torso taut and his eyes absolutely smoldering. "Thanks, Abby. I know this is going to work. I can *feel* it."

I glance down at his crotch. It's bulging like crazy. "Are you going to watch that video of me after I leave?"

"The minute I close the door."

My clit is throbbing. "Have fun."

"Oh, I will. Nighty-night, Assassin." He winks, flashes me a cocky grin, and slowly shuts the door.

I stand frozen in the hallway for a moment, staring at the soft yellow light shining through the peephole in the door, feeling like my very molecules are vibrating. Holy shit. I've agreed to have sex with a dude I've never met while Lucas Ford watches and tries his mighty best to resist pulling me aside to screw me himself, all so I can ultimately have the privilege of having sex with my teenage fantasy before heartlessly rejecting him...and he's going to pay me thirteen thousand bucks for my services? *How the hell did I get here?*

I'm just about to turn away from the door and drag my ass down the hallway toward the elevator when the light streaming through the peephole abruptly darkens.

Oh, hello, Lucas.

Well, gosh, as long as my favorite perverted rock star is peeping at me, it would be rude not to give him a bit of a show, right? I lean my back against the wall, slide my fingers underneath my skirt and into my panties, and begin to touch myself, all while staring directly at the darkened peephole and imagining Lucas standing behind the door, his eye trained on me, his hand sliding up and down his hard shaft. And not a minute later, my body begins rippling and clenching from deep inside.

When the waves of my orgasm have subsided, the light behind the peephole is still darkened and I'm pretty sure I can hear heavy breathing on the other side of the door.

I pull my fingers out of myself and lick them slowly with a full, extended tongue, making sure my audience of one can plainly surmise my lingual assets.

I hear a deep, muffled moan behind the door, followed by a light thudding noise, and my blood begins to simmer.

Still leaning against the wall, I pull my skirt way up, yank my G-string down, spread my legs, and open my delicate folds with my thumb and index finger until my hard, pink clit is fully exposed in all its swollen glory.

"I want you to lick it," I say, staring into the peephole. "And when you do, I'm going to come for you like a rocket."

There's another slight thud behind the door and then a strangled moan.

I dip my fingers into myself one more time, making sure they come out well slathered, cross the hallway, and smear the physical evidence of my arousal onto the peephole glass.

I stare for about ten seconds at the smeared peephole, my breathing labored, my heart pounding in my ears. Finally, I wink, lick my lips slowly like they're covered in Lucas's cum, and strut down the hallway toward the elevator, swinging my hips like a James Bond vixen as I go.

CHAPTER FOURTEEN

"What happened?" Danica asks when I slip behind the front desk.

"It was incredible," I reply. "Lucas wrote a song about me. Well, I guess, a song *inspired* by me. He played it for me and I gushed about how brilliant it was—because, oh my God, it was brilliant—and then we ate BLTs and talked and talked."

"Shut. *Up.* What'd you talk about?"

"I told him the basics about myself. You know, about law school and where I grew up and stuff. And then he told me about his band and friends and record label. *And then he told me the story behind 'Shattered Hearts'!*"

"*He did not.* Tell me everything!"

"I can't. Sorry. He swore me to secrecy."

"Bitch!" Danica whispers, but her tone is affectionate.

"I felt like I'd won a date with a rock star in a contest or something. And you want to hear the craziest part? He said I inspired him so much to write that one song, he wants me to come up to his suite every night this week during The Dead Zone to chat with him. He said I'm his 'muse'! Ha! So I said, 'Well, it might be kinda tough for me to get away every night while I'm on duty.' *So he said he'd pay me to do it!*"

Danica's face bursts into flames of jealousy. "Lucas Ford's going to *pay* you to sit there and *talk* with him?" Her eyes narrow suspiciously. "You slept with him, didn't you?"

"Of course not. Dani, come on, you know me. I'm a prude, remember? We didn't so much as kiss." It's a true statement, technically. Yes, I masturbated for him, licked splooge off his abs, and smeared my lady juices onto his peephole after he watched me masturbate for the second time, but I never actually kissed him.

Danica throws her head back dramatically. "Why, oh why, couldn't it have been *me* who told Lucas Ford not to smoke in the lobby? Gah! So how much is he going to pay you to sit there and 'inspire' him?"

"He offered me ten grand, but—"

"*Ten grand?*"

"But I figured, 'Hey, if he's *that* out of touch with reality, why not ask for a bit more and get the whole kit and caboodle for Danica's mom?' So I demanded thirteen. And he agreed!"

Danica looks like she's about to have a stroke.

"Thirteen grand is how much your mom owes on her medical bills, right?" I ask.

Danica clutches her chest and nods. "Are you sure?"

I touch Danica's hand. "One hundred percent."

"But what about your tuition and books?"

"Bah. I'm so in debt for school by now, thirteen grand wouldn't even make a dent. So why bother?"

Danica throws her arms around me and nuzzles her nose into my hair. "Thank you so much, Abby. I'll repay you some day, I swear."

"No repayment necessary. All I ask is you cover for me during

The Dead Zone when I go up to chat with him, okay?"

"Spend as much time up there as you want," Danica whispers into my hair, still squeezing me tight. "I've got your back 'til the end of time."

CHAPTER FIFTEEN

After a full morning of classes, I haul my exhausted ass into my tiny apartment, toss my backpack onto my couch, and drag myself into my kitchenette to make some scrambled eggs before heading off to bed. As exhausted as I am, though, I'm not holding out hope sleep will come quickly for me. I'm just too wound up with a thousand thoughts about what's going to happen later tonight. As willing as I am to have sex with Camden *once* to turn Lucas on and seduce him to seduce me—and, yes, admittedly also to experience a bit of kinky fun—I certainly don't want to make a career out of screwing Camden. This is a zero-sum game, after all. The more time I spend having sex with Camden, the less time will remain for my "relationship" with Lucas. And that's the realization that makes me ask myself on a running loop: What sneaky something can I do to light a fire under Lucas's ass to ensure he makes a move on me after only one go-around with Camden?

Unfortunately, I don't have an answer to that question yet, despite how obsessively I've been pondering it all day. But I'm sure as hell planning to have one before I walk into Lucas's penthouse tonight.

I finish scrambling my eggs and settle myself onto my couch to eat and unwind. First things first, I partake in my guilty pleasure. I grab my laptop and check the numbers on my secret blog—*Penelope Pleasure, Miss Pleasure to You!*—and I'm thrilled to see my latest entry has attracted my best numbers yet. I started my anonymous weekly blog of musings about life and sex with a humorous bent almost two years ago as a means of blowing off steam during law school, and I've been blown away at how it's steadily gained an army of loyal readers during that time.

I quickly write a short stream-of-consciousness post about the human emotion of *coveting* and how, it seems to me, it pretty much never ends well for either party—the coveter or the coveted. And when I'm done writing, I read my entry and feel almost high with pride about the finished product. There's literally no other place in this world where I can be unrelentingly honest about who I am and what I think than when I'm Penelope Pleasure. Truly, it's a lifeline for me.

Next on the agenda? Well, Lucas Ford, of course.

I head to YouTube and run a search for his name, and, of course, that brings up eighty gazillion video links, the first of which is, not surprisingly, Lucas's now-iconic music video for "Shattered Hearts." I personally adore it but haters always slam it as an extended Abercrombie & Fitch ad.

Even though probably one million of the over two billion views of the video were racked up by yours truly, I watch the thing again. And as I watch, my heart melts and flutters and leaps the way it always does when I behold the breathtaking beauty of an eighteen-year-old Lucas Ford pouring his shattered heart out for the entire world to witness.

When the video ends, I scroll through several more "Lucas

Ford" links and wind up watching a clip posted by someone in the front row of Lucas's concert in Denver a few days ago. At the start of the clip, Lucas is playing his electric guitar and singing a song I don't recognize while his full band—including Camden on drums—rocks out behind him. The song is really good, whatever it is, and by the passionate way Lucas is singing it, it's clear it means something special to him.

The song ends, and much to my dismay the audience applauds only tepidly.

Lucas wipes his sweaty brow, thanks the audience politely, and says, "So I've got one more song off my last album that I want to—"

But he's cut off by the person behind the recording device shouting, "'Shattered Hearts!'"

Darkness overtakes Lucas's beautiful features. He tries to smile but fails. "I'll get to that one," he assures the crowd. "But first I want to play something special to me I don't usually play off my third album—"

"'Shattered Hearts!'" the voice behind the camera commands again from the front row, and the sentiment is quickly seconded by another nearby audience member. And then another.

All of a sudden, a chant of "Shattered Hearts!" sweeps through the audience like a forest fire as Lucas stands frozen at his mic, clearly bewildered at how quickly the audience has rallied around their shared cause.

As the audience's chanting quickly gains momentum, Lucas's jaw noticeably tightens. "You want 'Shattered Hearts'?" he bellows into his microphone.

The audience roars at their victory, clearly missing the subtext of Lucas's booming query.

"You don't want me to play any song but 'Shattered Hearts'?" Lucas asks the crowd, his features hardening even further.

An avalanche of cheers and shouts of "Shattered Hearts!" slams into Lucas, making him visibly flinch.

The tortured look in Lucas's eyes is breaking my heart. How the hell does this audience not see the torment they're causing their supposed idol? I want to reach through my computer screen and hug him and say, "Play your song for *me*, Lucas."

"This sucks," Lucas mutters into his microphone, looking at his bass player, but the audience doesn't seem to hear him. Or maybe they just don't care. In a flash, rage ignites across Lucas's face. "Fuck you!" he shouts, flipping the audience off with both hands. He rips his guitar strap off, thrusts his instrument at his bass player, leans into his bass player's microphone, and shouts, "If you want to hear 'Shattered Hearts,' then listen to it on the goddamned radio. I'm done playing that fucking song forever." And off he goes, exiting the stage as the crowd unleashes a tsunami of boos and taunts at him.

After Lucas has disappeared, his band members remain awkwardly onstage, apparently not sure if their fearless leader is planning to return. The crowd absolutely explodes with fury and indignation. Whoever's behind the device that's recording yells, "Fuck you, Lucas Ford! You're washed up, anyway!" and then the video abruptly ends.

I touch my fingertip against my screen, right against the spot Lucas's tortured face occupied a moment ago. "Lucas," I whisper, my heart panging. *That's* what Lucas endured mere hours before he dragged himself into the lobby of The Rockford, slumped into an armchair, and got berated by a haughty hotel clerk about the Colorado Clean Indoor Air Act of 2006?

With a heavy sigh, I grab my phone, open iTunes, and download Lucas's third album. The album I never bothered to purchase three years ago because I'd heard someone say it was a "sharp departure" from Lucas's previous music and "not nearly as catchy."

I grab my earbuds, intending to listen to Lucas's album from top to bottom, but an incoming call on my phone interrupts my agenda. *Mom.*

CHAPTER SIXTEEN

"Hi, Mom," I say, picking up her call. "How are you?"

"Are you okay?" Mom asks.

"Yeah, I'm fine," I say, trying to make my voice sound like I'm fine.

"You sound upset."

"No, I'm good." I wipe my eyes. "I'm just exhausted, that's all."

"Did you go to class this morning?"

"Yup. Environmental law followed by employment law. Plus, I worked a full shift last night at the hotel before my classes and studied at the school's library in between. I'm about to take a quick shower and head off to bed before starting it all over again tonight. Welcome to my glamorous life. So what's up?"

"Oh, nothing. I'm just calling to say hi." Mom proceeds to tell me she's decided to redecorate the lake house again and that she's agreed to organize a charity gala for a hospital.

"Sounds great," I say, my eyelids heavy.

But Mom's not nearly done talking. She goes on for a while about how the new maid she hired to replace the old one—who retired after eleven years of loyal service—is sweet as can be but doesn't seem to possess enough attention to detail for her liking, which is a real pity, seeing as how Mom's got particularly high standards for cleanliness.

"Sounds like a first-world problem, Mom."

"Well, I didn't say it was a tragedy. I'm just giving you a rundown of my life." She pauses. "Are you sure you're okay? You sound a bit off."

"I'm fine."

"So are there any handsome future lawyers in your new classes this semester?"

"Yes, a few, but nobody I'm even remotely attracted to," I say, and instantly regret it. *Shit.* Why do I constantly poke the snake? I'm pathological.

"Abby," Mom says, years of exasperation with me instantly boiling to the surface. "*Please* try to give nice boys a chance for once. Would that be so hard?"

"I'm sorry, Mom," I say. "I'm just cranky because I'm tired. The truth is I don't have time to date anyone these days, whether they're a 'nice' future lawyer or a diabolical rock star." *Unless the rock star's Lucas Ford, of course, and then I've got all the time in the world.*

I can almost hear my mother's furrowed brow across the phone line. "Well, that's not healthy, either. You've got to have a little fun. Have you considered making an appointment with Dr. Carlson, just to check in?" she asks. "A little tune-up might be in order."

"I don't need therapy, Mom. I haven't had an issue in years."

"What would be the harm in a little check-in? Better safe than sorry."

"It'd be a colossal waste of my time and money, both of which are in short supply these days."

Mom makes a sound of complete exasperation. "Oh, Abigail, let's *please* not talk about the money thing again. You know Daddy's and my thoughts on that."

"Mom, I wasn't talking about money. I was only trying to say—"

"One day, you'll thank Daddy and me for not giving you a handout for your education. Daddy didn't get a handout from *his* parents and look what he wound up doing all on his own. It's like Daddy always says, people value a thing so much more when they scratch and claw to pay for it themselves."

"I wasn't implying I need or want your money," I say evenly. "I was simply trying to explain why I don't need more therapy, that's all. It'd be a pointless exercise because I already know exactly what we'd both say in the session. I'd say, 'Hi, Dr. Carlson. Yes, I still lead an excruciatingly boring life. Yes, I'm still making healthy choices. Every day. Yes, I'm still fully committed to respecting myself and my body and I understand my sexuality isn't a weapon that should be brandished to conquer men, especially not unattainable or unavailable ones. Rather, sex is something special that should be engaged in by two adult people in order to create intimacy as part of a committed relationship.' I'd say all that and Dr. Carlson would reply 'Wonderful, Abigail! Keep it up!' and then I'd pay her an exorbitant amount of money and leave. I truly can't fathom what would be the point of going to all that trouble when I can give myself an hour's worth of therapy for free."

"And here we are right back to money again."

"What? Mom, no. That's not what I meant. Are you listening to me at all?"

"Well, regardless, you know what Dr. Carlson says. You have *triggers*, Abby. Hit one of them hard enough on any given day and the floodgates might burst wide open on you."

"My floodgates are firmly battened down, Mom. Don't worry. They can't possibly open even a crack when all I do is work, study, and sleep. Gimme a fucking break."

"Abigail!" my mother gasps. "I will not tolerate that kind of language from you."

I really am pathological. Why do I constantly do this? "I'm sorry, Mom. It just slipped out. I'm sleep-deprived. Forgive me. Please, don't start thinking one F-bomb is a sign the 'floodgates' are opening. They're not, okay? I'm battened down and buttoned up and making healthy choices every day of my life."

There's a long, awkward silence.

"Mom, please don't worry about me. I know I put you and Daddy through a lot, and as I've said a thousand times, I'm genuinely sorry about all that. But that was a long time and many therapy sessions ago. I'm twenty-four now, not nineteen. I've got my head on straight, I promise."

Mom sighs with relief. "I'm glad to hear it." Her voice breaks. "I only worry because I love you so much."

A lump rises in my throat. "I know. I love you, too. And Daddy. Will you tell him I said 'hi'? I texted him yesterday and he hasn't replied."

"Oh, that's because he's in London on business. I'm sure he'll call you when he's got a minute."

"That'd be great. Okay, well, I'd better get some sleep. I've got to work another full shift again tonight."

"All right, darling. Sweet dreams."

"Thanks, Mom. I love you."

I hang up the phone and bring my half-empty plate of eggs into my kitchenette. I wash and dry my plate and put it neatly away, take out the trash, scrub my counters and pan, and then drag my tired ass into the bathroom for a shower.

Hot water pelts my sore shoulders and back, and my mind wanders. I don't mean to do it, but I start thinking about how much pain I've caused my parents in my short lifetime. How much embarrassment. And then I think about how tired I am. How tired I *always* am. And, finally, I think about the tortured expression on Lucas's face when the audience at his Denver concert demanded he perform the one song he simply doesn't feel like playing ever again.

When I'm done showering, I slip into my pajamas and fuzzy socks, pull down the shades in my bedroom to block out the glorious, sunny day beckoning me, and lay my weary head on my pillow. Finally, I'm snuggled nice and cozy in my bed. I put an eye mask on, push earbuds into my ears, and press play on the first song on Lucas's third album, letting Lucas's beautiful, soulful voice usher me into blissful sleep.

CHAPTER SEVENTEEN

I stand in front of the door to Penthouse A, clutching Lucas's signed non-disclosure agreement in my hand, my jaw clenched. On the drive into work, I had a brilliant idea about how to get Lucas to claim me sooner rather than later. And now I'm bound and determined to execute on my strategy.

I take a deep breath, shake out my arms, and knock on the door...and not ten seconds later Camden Donnelly's standing in the doorway.

Holy hell, Camden's an attractive guy—even more so than that video of him playing drums led me to believe. He's got strawberry-blond hair, blazing blue eyes, muscles, tattoos, and facial hair. Most importantly, he's got *swagger*. I've got to think there aren't too many situations in life where Camden Donnelly considers himself any girl's consolation prize.

"Hey, Abby," Camden says, his voice low and masculine. He leans forward and kisses me gently on the cheek like he's done it a thousand times, and my skin pricks at the sensation of his short beard and soft lips against my flesh. I inhale deeply before he retracts from me and take in the scent of him. Soap. Faint cologne. Nice.

I open my mouth to reply to Camden, but my brain is hijacked when I spot Lucas over his shoulder, inside the suite, staring at me with eyes like a sniper's. I look at Camden again and smile for Lucas's benefit. "Hey, *baby*," I say, speaking loud enough for Lucas to overhear. "I've been fantasizing about you all day. In fact, I've already gotten myself off twice today watching a video of you pounding away on the drums."

Camden's eyebrows shoot up.

"Gimme a kiss, baby," I say. "I've missed you so much."

Camden leans forward and whispers, "You're sure you're okay with all this?"

I take a step forward, slide my arms around Camden's neck, and press my body into his. "I'm great with it," I whisper. And then, at full voice, I add, "Kiss me, Cammy. I've been aching all day to kiss you."

Camden makes a face that says, "Why the fuck not?" and then, without further ado, he wraps his muscled arms around me and lays a gentle introductory kiss on my lips. And then another. And another. And when my lips tell him I'm a willing and enthusiastic partner, he gets down to business, opening my mouth with his lips and introducing his tongue to mine with languid, sensual swirling motions.

Wow. This is a surprisingly pleasant kiss. Camden tastes minty and fresh. He smells lovely. And, most of all, the movements of his lips and tongue against mine are confident but not overbearing. The whole experience is highly arousing, actually. I press myself into Camden's body with increased fervor and grind my crotch against his, and I'm rewarded with the sensation of his steely hard-on.

Without hesitation, I reach down and gently stroke his bulge. He jolts with surprise at my touch but then presses himself into my hand and lets out a little moan of excitement as he continues to kiss me. I stroke his hard-on enthusiastically, and he slides his hands down my back and gropes my ass, a move that prompts me to work his bulge with even more zeal.

Camden lets out a soft noise that tells me what I'm doing is working mighty fine for him, thank you very much, and our kiss ramps up even more until we're basically standing in the doorframe dry humping each other. Holy crap, this is unexpected. And insanely exciting. I can honestly say whatever trepidation I might have had about this bizarre game is long gone now, just this fast. If Camden screws like he kisses, I'm in for a delicious treat.

Finally, Camden's hungry lips lead mine to closing and he disengages from our kiss.

I open my eyes, still stroking the intoxicating bulge in his pants, and flash him a beaming smile.

"Jesus Christ," he says, pressing himself into my hand. "Your motor runs hot as hell, huh?"

I nod vigorously and grip his hard dick. "White-hot," I reply— again, loud enough for my audience of one to overhear me. I steal a quick peek at Lucas, eager to find out if he's been watching and *coveting* me like a good boy...and it's quite clear to me that, yes, he most certainly has. Lucas is absolutely rooted to his spot, his eyes on fire, looking like he wants to fuck me more than he wants to breathe. Well, either that, or he's a serial killer who's plotting his next kill.

I resist the urge to wink at Lucas. *Careful what you wish for, sweetheart.*

"You're completely sure you're up for this?" Camden whispers, drawing my attention back to him in the doorway. "Luke wants us to stay in character. No breaks, ever."

I nod. "Go for it. Let's give our boy a sexy show and have a little kinky fun for ourselves in the process."

Camden's smile is positively wicked. "My thoughts exactly." He grabs my hand, leads me into the suite, and speaks at full volume again: "You want a drink before I fuck the living hell out of you, beautiful?" he asks.

"Thanks, love. I'd love one."

Camden deposits me onto the couch with a passionate kiss, mere feet from where Lucas is standing, gawking at us, and then he strides toward the bar across the room, strutting like a man who's about to get laid. "Luke? You want a drink, brother?"

"Thanks," Lucas mutters, his dark eyes fixed on me. Jesus God, the way he's looking at me, I can't tell if he wants to kiss, fuck, or murder me. Frankly, I'm so turned on, I'd be game for any of it.

"Hi, Lucas," I say, my eyes locked with his. I pointedly hold up the envelope with the signed NDA inside it and toss it onto the coffee table.

Lucas nods his acknowledgment of the contract. "Hi, Abby," he replies, his eyes on fire. He points to the coffee table where there's an envelope with the word "Assassin" scrawled across it, and I nod my acknowledgment of the first half of my payment. He sits down in an armchair across from me and immediately shifts his hard-on in his jeans. "How are you this fine evening, Assassin?"

"Horny," I reply. "And happy to see my boyfriend. I've been aching for him all day."

Lucas's jaw muscles pulse. He doesn't reply.

"Cheers, guys," Camden says, returning with whiskey shots and beers. The three of us knock back our shots and clink our beers, and then Camden seats himself next to me on the couch, grabs my face, and kisses me like I'm oxygen and he's a drowning man.

Well, all righty then. Here we go.

I hike up my navy-blue pencil skirt to allow free movement of my thighs, climb aboard the SS Camden and straddle his lap. "I'm aching for you, Cammy," I say, my palms on his cheeks, my crotch grinding into his bulge, my bare ass jutting out of my raised skirt to give Lucas a show. "I'm so wet for you, baby. Feel how wet I am for you."

I don't need to ask Camden Donnelly twice. He glides his hand down my ass crack along the path forged by my G-string, and when he reaches the crotch of my itty-bitty panties, he slips his fingers underneath the fabric and straight inside of me.

I shift my body to give Camden a better angle on fingering me and he lets out a groan of excitement. "You're soaking wet," he says, his fingers dipping into me with enthusiasm. "Jesus, it's like I've gone down on you, you're so wet."

I'm dying to know what Lucas is doing behind me and what his face looks like right now. But that's okay. A girl can imagine. With visions of Lucas's blazing face flashing across my mind, I begin humping Camden's hand slowly and methodically, sliding my swollen clit against his finger to drive myself wild. "Oh, God, that feels good," I whisper.

"You like that?" Camden says softly, his voice laced with desire.

"You know I do. Do you feel how wet I am for you?"

"I sure do."

"Will you lick me, baby?" I breathe, snapping my pelvis against Camden's hand with precision. "If you lick me, I'll return the favor and suck your dick like it's made of the finest chocolate."

Camden lets out a shaky breath. "You got yourself a deal, baby. Fuck yeah."

In one fluid motion, Camden tosses me onto my back on the couch like I'm a blow-up doll—a maneuver that allows me to glance over at Lucas...and I lose my freaking mind at the sight of him. Oh my God, Lucas looks unbelievably hot right now. He's gripping the arms of his chair with white knuckles, his eyes burning like hot coals and the bulge behind his jeans massive. And, I must say, it's a sexy look for him.

Camden pulls off his shirt, attracting my attention back to him, and my jaw drops. *Wow*. I had no idea Camden was hiding such a gorgeous body underneath that shirt!

Without hesitation, Camden pulls off my shirt, and then my skirt, followed by my matching black bra and G-string, leaving me lying before him buck naked and trembling.

"Nice," Camden says, his eyes scorching a path from my hard nipples to my belly ring and finally landing with obvious approval on the tiny angel tattoo gracing my pubic bone. "Well, look at you," Camden says, his eyes blazing. "You're full of surprises, aren't you?"

I sneak a quick peek at Lucas to find him breathing like he just ran a hundred-yard dash, still gripping the arms of his chair.

I focus on Camden again. His jeans are off. He's wearing black boxer briefs and his hard-on is straining deliciously behind the fabric.

"Oh, Cammy," I coo. "I've been fantasizing about you doing this to me all day."

"Your wish is my command," Camden whispers. He moves

between my legs and...shit! No! This new positioning of Camden's body is blocking my view of Lucas! But before I can panic, Lucas appears in my sightline again. The sneaky bastard's switched chairs to ensure he doesn't miss a moment of our sexy show.

I can't help smiling broadly as I return my gaze to the man between my legs. The man who's currently kissing my breasts and sucking on my hard nipples.

"I want you so much, Camden," I purr, reaching down and stroking the hard-on behind his briefs. "I'm already so close." I turn my head and look straight at Lucas—one hand working my clit while the other strokes Camden—and my entire body jolts as I discover Lucas's jeans unbuttoned and the tip of his hard cock emerging from the waistband of his white underwear. An involuntary moan escapes my mouth at this unexpected glimpse of Lucas's smooth, shiny tip. I arch my back, suddenly aching almost painfully to get fucked. "I'm so turned on," I whisper with my eyes fixed on Lucas as Camden's tongue works its way down my torso toward my throbbing tip. "You're so good at this, Camden."

With his dark eyes still trained on mine, Lucas pulls the full length of his hard dick and his balls out of his briefs and begins slowly stroking his shaft. Not three seconds later, Camden's warm, wet tongue lands on my clit and begins fervently licking me, exactly the way I like it best.

I'm suddenly experiencing a perfect storm of turn-ons. Enough wicked pleasure to make a girl like me come forcefully, just that fast. I make a primal sound, arch my back sharply, shove myself into Camden's warm mouth, and come shockingly hard, my eyes never leaving Lucas's.

LAUREN ROWE

"Oh, yeah, baby," Camden says into my cooch, his lips devouring me.

"Keep going." I gasp, gripping Camden's hair. "I'll come again even harder if you keep going."

Camden doubles down on what he's doing and I moan loudly. Damn, Camden's definitely good at this. I grip Camden's hair even harder and begin riding his mouth, continuing to stare at Lucas's beautiful, tortured, turned-on face.

Lucas.

He's absolutely gorgeous right now.

He's stroking himself as he watches Camden and me. But he's working himself slowly, like he doesn't want to push himself too close to the edge. I lick my lips, imagining myself sucking him off as Camden's tongue continues working its magic on my clit. "So good," I purr, not taking my eyes off Lucas. "So, so good. Oh, God. I'm almost there again, Cam. Keep doing it just like that, love. Don't stop doing exactly that."

"You taste amazing," Camden says from between my legs, his enthusiasm seemingly quite sincere.

Oh my hell, this dude between my legs is a talented individual. I'm on the cusp of complete rapture. But I can't let go. Not yet. I need to hang on until I've given Lucas enough reason to push Camden off me and claim me for himself.

Camden's continuing to chow down on me like a starving man.

And Lucas is beating himself off with languid jerks of his hand, his eyes fixed on mine.

And me? I'm on the verge of coming undone.

I cling to control, forcing myself not to release. But when Lucas

119

licks his lips in an exaggerated swirl, showing me exactly how he'd eat me out if he were the one hunkered down between my legs, I lose it and come into Camden's mouth for a second time, this time much more forcefully than the first.

"Oh, fuck, yes," I grit out as my body warps and wrenches with a tsunami of pleasure, still looking at Lucas. "You're amazing, Camden. The best."

Once my orgasm has subsided, I grip Camden's hair and pull him up to my face for a long, deep kiss, making sure he can't shove his dick into my mouth, despite what I promised him earlier. "Baby," I coo to Camden. "You've got me so turned on, I want to do something extra sexy that's going to make sucking your dick especially hot for me."

Camden leans back slightly, his chest heaving, waiting to hear whatever this crazy bitch he just met fifteen minutes ago is about to say to him.

I put my palms on Camden's scruffy cheeks, wrap my naked thighs around him, and grind myself into the bulge behind his briefs. "You know how you've been begging me for a threesome forever? Well, I'm finally ready to do it because you got me off so hard and I love you so much. In fact, I'm *dying* to do it for you—*as my gift to you.*"

Camden's eyes are wide. He tries to glance over at Lucas, but I pull his face toward me by his scruff.

"I know how much you love to be in charge when we fuck, so don't worry, I promise whoever you pick to be our plaything will be yours to command. Nothing but a toy for me—a human dildo."

Camden chuckles and glances at Lucas, an amused look on his

face that plainly says, "She's clever."

It's taking all my self-restraint not to join Camden in looking at Lucas, but I force myself not to do it, for the greater good. What better way to make a rock star feel compelled to elbow his way to center stage than making him feel like nothing but part of the measly backup band?

I pull Camden's scruff again and make him look at me. "This is your show, babe. You'll tell our toy when to fuck me and how hard and how fast or slow. You'll tell him if and when he's allowed to come. And the whole time, I'll be sucking you off better than you've ever had, I promise. Baby, you haven't been blown 'til you've been blown by me."

Camden's eyes blaze. "I'm sold," he whispers. "Let's do it."

"Command me." I look at Lucas. "*Sir*."

At my use of that particular word, Lucas looks like he's about to explode, but he remains seated, his hand slowly working his shaft and his chest heaving.

Camden stands, scoops my naked body off the couch with his muscled arms, and strides with his girlfriend-for-the-night toward the bedroom, his dick straining behind his black briefs. "Come on, Human Dildo," he calls over his shoulder to his rock star best friend. "Whatever my sexy girl wants, she gets. *Including you*."

CHAPTER EIGHTEEN

Camden's naked and kneeling at the head of the bed, his massive hard-on mere inches from my lips.

I'm naked and on all fours on the mattress, my back swayed and my bare ass protruding toward the true object of my affection—who, at the moment, is sitting fully dressed in an armchair in the corner, the tip of his hard-on peeking out the top of his unbuttoned jeans.

"Suck my dick, Abby," Camden whispers, his fingertips stroking my hair. "If you want to get fucked by a human dildo, you've got to earn it."

I nod, lick my lips, and get to work.

I start by licking Camden's dick from his balls to his tip like he's a melting Popsicle. My fingers explore his balls and taint as I work, my lips and tongue voracious, and when it's clear he's appropriately turned on, I move along to lapping enthusiastically at Camden's tip—a maneuver that prompts him to grip my hair and moan his appreciation.

I'm about to take Camden's full cock into my mouth when he surprises me by barking out, "Strip down and get over here, Dildo."

My mouth involuntarily freezes. *Holy shit. This is it.*

Camden strokes my hair. "Keep going, beautiful. The better you suck me off, the more I'll order him to do to you."

Well, hell. Sounds like a fair trade-off to me.

I take Camden's tip into my mouth again and swirl my tongue over his little hole while my fingers continue exploring him, anxiously awaiting the feel of Lucas's hands on my flesh for the very first time. But nope. I feel nothing.

All right. Time to get Camden lobbying for me.

I take Camden's full length into my mouth while continuing to swirl my tongue on his tip, and almost instantly the dude begins losing his mind. Wow, Camden's damned easy to please in the blowjob department, it seems. Could it be his famewhore of a girlfriend isn't a big fan of giving head? Well, shame on her if her man likes it so much. Give your man what he likes, I say. And lots of it.

"Holy fuck, you're good at this," Camden grits out. "Luke, she's amazing at this, man. Fuck."

I increase the speed and intensity of my assault and Camden's entire body shudders. And then I slide my fingertip into his ass crack and—

"Dildo!" Camden suddenly barks at Lucas. "Get over here and lick my girl's asshole."

My heart lurches. If Lucas complies, this will be the first time he'll lay a hand—or tongue—on me. And holy hell, Camden sure picked a doozy of a first touch.

To my thrill, as I continue sucking Camden's dick and fondling him, the mattress behind me lowers sharply with Lucas's body weight.

And then I feel Lucas's warm palms rest on my ass cheeks.

Lucas strokes my ass for a long, delicious moment, making me shudder, and then moves on to stroking the outside of my pussy gently, making me quake with anticipation.

I feel Lucas's fingers gently spreading my ass cheeks apart...and then the sensation of Lucas's warm lips and tongue on my asshole...which he then proceeds to lick and eat like it's covered in maple syrup.

Holy fuckburgers.

I attack Camden's dick with animalistic ferocity, and Camden jerks and bucks into my mouth like he's being electrocuted.

"Finger her pussy while you eat her," Camden barks at Lucas. "Oh, fuck, she's incredible. Make her lose her mind for me, Luke."

Still eating my ass, Lucas begins fingering my clit, and just like that I'm so turned on I'm no longer human. And Camden's right there with me. He grips my hair and begins face-fucking me as Lucas continues his assault on my ass and clit.

Oh, good lord. This is intense. And side note? I'm pretty sure if Dr. Carlson were here, she'd tell me this isn't a "healthy choice."

I make a garbled sound—as best I can with Camden's cock down my throat—on the bitter edge of a brutal release, and try my damnedest to hang on.

"Fuck her slow," Camden chokes out to Lucas, his balls slamming into my chin. "I can't hold on much longer. Fuck her slow and tell me what she feels like."

Lucas roughly grabs my hips and without a moment's hesitation burrows his massive hard-on inside me, a maneuver that elicits simultaneous groans of excitement from all three of us.

"Oh, fuck, Cam, she's really tight," Lucas grits out, fucking me slowly. "Jesus Christ, man, she feels so fucking good."

"Fuck her hard and finger her," Camden orders, his voice

strained. "Make her come. Oh, fuck, this is good."

Lucas follows his best friend's orders to a tee, a move that makes me wail with pleasure and attack Camden's dick with increased fervor.

"Oh, Jesus," Camden bellows. "Baby, don't stop."

I've never felt so much dirty pleasure in my life. I let out a guttural groan.

"I can't hang on much longer," Lucas chokes out.

"Wait for me," Camden orders. "Me first. She's mine."

"Fuck!" Lucas shouts. "She feels incredible, man. Oh my God."

Apparently, that's too much for Camden to bear. With a loud growl, he pulls out of my mouth and comes all over my face, a shocking denigration that causes my core to release with a wrenching, brutal orgasm of such force, fluid gushes out of me and spurts around Lucas's massive cock and onto my thighs.

"Oh, God," Lucas chokes out, just before pulling out of me and releasing all over my ass.

I collapse onto the mattress along with Camden while Lucas crumples onto the edge of the bed. For several moments, the three of us remain motionless and mute, gasping for air.

"Well, that was messy," I finally say, and everyone breaks into hearty laughter.

"You're a unicorn, Abby," Camden says, still laughing. "How do you exist?"

"No, man," Lucas says. "She's not a *unicorn*." Without warning, he bites my ass cheek—*hard*—making me gasp with surprise. "*She's an angel*."

CHAPTER NINETEEN

I slip behind the front desk. "Sorry I took so long," I say to Danica. "Thanks for holding down the fort."

"How'd it go?"

"Great. We just talked and talked. It's so weird. We have these great conversations, but there's no sexual chemistry at all. Lucas says he really appreciates the chance to talk with a woman without any sexual undertones. I don't think he's used to having many female friends."

Danica's facial expression tells me she's buying everything I'm selling, without question—which kind of pisses me off, actually. "That's so sweet," she says. "Why is the front of your hair wet?"

My chest tightens. Obviously, I can't tell Danica I took a quick shower in Lucas's suite before heading back down to work. "Because I had to wash my face before I left," I say smoothly. "Lucas was so excited about a new song he wrote, he shook up a bottle of champagne and opened it and it sprayed all over me." I roll my eyes. "I was actually annoyed with him."

Again, Danica looks completely convinced. "So he wants you back again tomorrow night?"

"Yup. Same time. Okay with you?"

"Sure thing." She smiles sheepishly. "Okay, so don't be mad at me, but I didn't even start working on the P and R reports yet. Sorry, I got distracted. I was hoping you'd start working on them while I take my break and grab some food?"

"Of course. Take as long as you need. Thanks so much for covering for me for so long."

"You bet." Danica pinches my butt as she moves around the front desk, her fingers squeezing an inch away from the spot where Lucas bit me so unexpectedly mere minutes ago. "See ya in about forty-five?" Danica asks.

"Great."

Danica leaves and I begin dutifully working on the P&R reports, but about ten minutes into my work I'm interrupted by an incoming call on the main board from Penthouse A.

"Why, hello there, Mr. Ford. Or should I call you Count Dracula?"

Lucas chuckles. "How's your tasty ass?"

"It hurts."

"Sorry about that. Got carried away. Is that why you left so damned fast?"

"Of course not. I just had to get back to work."

"Yeah, but you didn't have to bolt outta here like the place was on fire. You sure you're okay?"

"I'm fine."

"You're not freaking out?"

"Not at all. I'm great."

"Good. I thought maybe you left like that because you were freaking out and wanted to quit the game."

"I'm not freaking out at all," I say. "And I don't want to quit the game in the slightest."

I can hear his smile across the phone line. "Good." He sighs. "God, that was hot, wasn't it? *Damn,* Abby."

Heat spreads to my core. "Yeah, it was pretty hot."

"You're a savage beast, woman. I've done plenty of threesomes before—although always with two women—but holy mother of God, they've never been anything close to as hot as what we just did. Camden and I were talking about it after you left, and we both agreed it was because of *you.* You come off as this sweet little virgin, which is pretty sexy in itself, not going to lie, and then bam! It turns out you're hiding a devil underneath your halo and wings. Best of both worlds." He chuckles. "I honestly hadn't even thought about throwing a threesome into the mix for our game. You definitely ambushed me with that—" He abruptly stops talking and inhales sharply like he's been stuck with a needle.

"Lucas?"

"Holy shit. Hang on. I just had an epic idea for a song. Holy fuck! Hang on, baby. I've got to write something down before I forget it."

There's silence on the line for a full minute.

"Sorry about that," he says when he gets back on the line. "What were we talking about?"

"You were saying I ambushed you with the threesome."

"Oh, yeah. Sorry. Holy fuck, I'm bouncing off the walls right now. I feel high. God, that was incredible."

Crap. I'm beginning to think maybe I've miscalculated here. I introduced the threesome element into our role-play with the goal of breaking the seal with Lucas, so to speak, thinking he'd get a taste of me and immediately want me for himself. But, unfortunately,

Lucas doesn't sound at all like a man who wants to claim me as his girlfriend. He sounds like a man who just had a hell of a great time in a threesome and wants to do it again. "Well, glad you and Camden had so much fun," I say flatly, my stomach clenching.

Lucas pauses. "But you did, too, right?"

I don't reply.

"Oh, shit. You're *pissed*?" he says.

I remain mute, but only because I don't know what to say. I'm not pissed, actually. I'm...vaguely disappointed my little scheme didn't work. But I don't know how to explain that to Lucas without sounding like an extremely manipulative little bitch.

"What are you pissed about?" Lucas asks. "You obviously got off on what we did every bit as much as Camden and I did. I mean, either that or you're a porn-star version of Meryl Streep."

I can't help myself. I chuckle. "Well, yeah, obviously I got off on it. No acting skills, no matter how masterful, could make a woman shoot cum out her cooch."

Lucas guffaws at that.

"Lucas, the truth is, I only suggested the threesome to light a fire under your ass. I did it to make you want me for yourself, not to make you want to blurt, 'Hey, Camden, let's make Abby our penis pincushion again!'"

Lucas laughs. "Yeah, I already knew that's why you did it. I'm not stupid, Abby. And don't worry. It worked like a charm."

"It did?"

"Of course, it did. Why do you think I bit your ass? I was claiming you, baby. You're all mine now."

My heart leaps. "I am?"

"Fuck yeah. Just like you planned. Now that I've had you, there's no going back. You're a diabolical genius, babe.'"

I want to shriek with glee but I somehow manage to contain myself. "So it's going to be me and you from now on, then?"

"Well, yeah, you're mine now, for sure. But if it's all right with you, I was kind of thinking it'd be fun to do the threesome thing with Camden once more—but with me in charge of my girlfriend's pleasure. How about we use Cam as our human dildo and I get my girl off even harder next time?"

I consider that idea for a moment. Truthfully, it sounds hot as hell. The devil on my shoulder is nodding profusely. But the angel? That little bitch keeps hearing Dr. Carlson's voice whispering in her ear.

"You still there?" Lucas asks.

"Yeah, I'm just thinking about it."

"Hey, no thinking allowed."

I remain mute, still lost in a tug-of-war inside my own mind.

"Hey, how about you come up here and talk this through with me?" he says. "I think this is the kind of conversation we should have face-to-face."

"I wish I could, but I'm all alone down here. Danica took her break."

"There's no one in the lobby but you?"

"It's just little ol' me."

"No guests?"

"Nope. The first checkouts won't start happening for another thirty minutes or so, I'd guess."

"Okay, cool. Hang tight. I'm coming down to see you to help you figure this out."

Before I can reply, the line goes dead. Four minutes later, one of the elevators opens and Lucas strides out in all his rock star glory, his face positively glowing. "Hello, Angel," he says brightly when he reaches the front desk.

My heart leaps at the sight of his gorgeousness. "Hello, Mr. Ford," I reply. "Wow, you look happy."

"I am." He leans his elbow on the counter and shoots me a boyish smile. "You know why I'm happy? On the way down here in the elevator, *another* killer song came to me. I can't wait to race back upstairs and write it."

Oh my gosh, he's absolutely adorable right now. "Is it another 'Shattered Hearts'?" I ask hopefully.

"Nope. I'm not even close to writing that motherfucker yet. This one's going to be a pretty love song for my pretty, perverted girl who looks like an angel and fucks like the devil."

I look around to confirm nobody's entering the lobby. "How about you kiss your pretty, perverted girl for an extra jolt of inspiration?"

"Nope. I'm dying to kiss you for the first time, don't get me wrong, but when I do, I want to do it right. Kissing's a much bigger deal to me than fucking, actually. That's why I didn't kiss Camden's girlfriend. It means something to me."

"So does that mean I won't be kissing Camden again?"

He nods. "Damn straight. Only me."

"And yet you still want another threesome?"

"With me in the driver's seat and Camden as our toy." He shrugs. "But like I said before, if you feel uncomfortable at any time, you say so and we stop. I just figured you'd be up for it, since you're the one who suggested the threesome in the first place." He looks at me sideways like he thinks he's calling my bluff in a game of poker.

I consider my reply for a moment. "Frankly, I'm up for doing anything with you, if you genuinely want it. And as long as you're genuinely feeling inspired by it. That's what we're here to do, right? Help you *feel* again after so many years of being shut down?"

Lucas smiles broadly. "You're amazing, Abby, you know that? An angel. I've never met anyone who looks so innocent on the one hand, but who's—" He abruptly stops talking. His face lights up. "Oh, *shit*. I just had *another* song idea! Oh, Jesus, I've got to get back upstairs and start writing. I'm a volcano erupting! Ha! I'll see you tomorrow night, okay, baby?" He blows me a kiss. "See you tomorrow."

I wave. "Happy songwriting."

Lucas takes a step away from me but abruptly whirls around to face me again. "Hey, by the way, I don't want you bolting away again tomorrow night, okay? It freaked me out. I know you've got to work but I truly thought you hated me when you left."

"Hated you? What part of me gushing fluid out my cooch made you think I *hated* you?"

He rolls his eyes. "Well, not that part, obviously. Just the part when you ran away. It felt like, I dunno, maybe you were...ashamed?"

I consider that idea for a long beat and realize it's true. "Yeah, I think I was a bit ashamed," I admit. "But not in the way you think. I think I felt ashamed by how much I liked what we did. Not by the fact that I did the deed in the first place."

Lucas's beautiful smile broadens. "Now see? I couldn't have come up with a sexier response than that in my hottest fantasies. Ha!

That's why you're my muse, baby. Because I couldn't make this shit up if I tried. Who else but you could possibly bring a sexy meaning to the word 'ashamed'?" His face lights up again. "Oh, for the love of fuck! I just got *another* song idea!" He lurches forward across the counter like he's going to leap across it and kiss the hell out of me, but he stops short and cups my face in his palms, smiling like a lunatic. "Never feel ashamed of who you are. You hear me? So you're a girl who likes to fuck and does it well. So what? You think Camden and I feel ashamed of what we did? Not for a minute. So, start thinking like a dude and own who you are. You're perfect just the way you are. And don't let anybody tell you any differently." With that, he releases my face, slides off the counter, winks, and strides with breathtaking swagger toward the elevator bank, leaving me standing alone behind the front desk with my knees weak and my heart in my mouth.

CHAPTER TWENTY

I can't concentrate on what my professor at the front of the lecture hall is saying. Employment law is my favorite class, actually, but today nothing can compete with my daydreams about what depraved and perverted things are undoubtedly going to happen to me later tonight in the penthouse suite. I focus on my laptop screen and realize I haven't typed a single word since my professor started talking over twenty minutes ago.

Oh, well, I suppose if I'm not going to pay a lick of attention today in class, I should use my time for something more fulfilling than staring off into space. I click into my blog and begin writing a new entry about threesomes and the undeniable appeal of taboo sex in general. The minute I begin writing, my exhaustion melts away and the words pour out of me in a torrent of excitement. Much like how Lucas said he felt when he wrote "Assassin," I feel like I'm merely transcribing an essay already in existence in the universe.

When I'm done writing, I sit back in my chair, pride welling up inside me. Wow, words have never just *flowed* out of me quite like this before. And, if I do say so myself, they were excellent words. The finished product is honest and raw. Vulnerable and funny. And sexy as hell. Of course, if my parents ever found out about this essay or my blog in general, they'd literally disown me, or maybe even try to get me institutionalized. But I don't care. I now realize this blog is my lifeline. The only place in the world where I'm free to be myself. And nothing in the world could make me give it up.

The professor wraps up class and tells us about our next reading assignment and I begin packing up my laptop and books.

"Hey, Abby," a male voice says.

I look up. *Noah.*

"I'm thinking about grabbing a burger," Noah says. "You want to join me?"

Oh, man, he looks so damned hopeful. But he's just not the man for me. "Thanks so much, Noah, but I worked a full shift at the hotel last night and I'm working again tonight, so I've got to get home and catch up on my sleep."

"When do you have another night off? Maybe I could take you out to a nice dinner? I was thinking maybe we could try a real date next time."

"I'm sorry," I say. "I've actually got a boyfriend now."

Noah's face falls. "Wow. That was quick. I thought you said you..." He shifts his backpack on his shoulder. "Is this the same guy you'd just gotten out of a relationship with the other night, or...?"

"No, no, it's someone completely different. Someone I've had a crush on for a long time. We finally connected out of nowhere the other night. The night after you and I got together, actually, and it was like, *ka-boom*! Fireworks. You know how that goes."

Noah's cheeks flush. "No, unfortunately, I don't."

My stomach clenches. This nice guy doesn't deserve a girl like me. He deserves a nice girl who'll appreciate him. But there's nothing I can do about it. I don't want him.

"I'm sorry," I squeak out. "It just happened out of the blue."

"No worries," Noah says. He tries to smile. "I hope it works out for you. Just do me a favor. Tell your new boyfriend, whoever he is, Noah Endicott says he's a lucky bastard."

CHAPTER TWENTY-ONE

I keep tossing and turning in bed in my darkened bedroom.

No matter how exhausted I am, I can't stop obsessing about what's going to happen later tonight at the hotel with Camden and Lucas. Now that I've had a little time to work through my thoughts about the situation, I'm certain I have no desire to engage in a replay of last night, even if the guys flip their roles and Lucas assumes control of whose dick goes where.

True, last night was unbelievably exciting, I can't deny that. But I think it was mostly because I was experiencing the rush of making Lucas do something he hadn't planned to do. *I was conquering him.* But am I really up for a planned orgy with both men, for no other reason than to satisfy our mutual depravity and with no psychological component beyond sheer hedonism? Honestly, I really don't think I am. *See, Mom? I told you I don't need Dr. Carlson anymore!*

The truth is, I want Lucas, not Camden. And as fun as last night's threesome was, and as much as I'll probably want to try one again at some point, right now, no amount of talking myself into screwing Camden again—even if Lucas is calling the shots—seems to be working.

I turn onto my opposite side in the bed. The problem is, every time I imagine myself in bed with both Lucas and Camden, I can't seem to settle on a parking spot for Camden's dick. Would I want him to shove his dick down my throat again? Um, no, thank you. Although I thoroughly enjoyed the way Camden unexpectedly wound up face-fucking me, it now feels like a one-time thing to me. Been there, done that. I'm absolutely positive I won't feel an equivalent thrill doing it exactly like that again.

So, okay, then I imagine Camden giving me a special delivery through my back door while Lucas simultaneously gives me one through my front, and I literally shudder at the thought. Would I like to get double-fucked by two men simultaneously one day? Hell yes, I would. Pretty please. But in this context, at this moment in time, it doesn't feel right. First off, anal is kind of special to me, actually. It definitely requires intense trust with my partner and lots of communication. I've only done it twice in my life, so I'm thinking Lucas, not Camden, should be the special guy who gets to claim my almost-virgin ass tonight. And yet, when I think, "Okay, so that leaves Lucas giving it to me up my ass while Camden fucks me up the cooch," that combination doesn't seem right, either. How the hell could I give *Camden* my sacred pussy and let him be the man who looks into my eyes while fucking me? The man who gets to kiss me and press his hard chest into my soft breasts while sliding himself in and out of me, all while Lucas, the man I want more than life itself, is once again left to fuck me anonymously from behind? It just doesn't feel right.

All of which leads me to the same conclusion again and again: I don't want to fuck Lucas *and* Camden tonight. I want Lucas and no one else. And, unfortunately, no matter how much I try to convince myself otherwise, no matter how much money Lucas is paying me, no matter how hard I got off last night with both guys, I simply can't seem to change the way I feel down deep in my soul.

Damn.

I guess all that therapy with Dr. Carlson managed to leave a mark on me, after all.

Crap.

CHAPTER TWENTY-TWO

I exit the elevator and walk down the hallway toward Penthouse A, my jaw set and my mind racing. What's going to happen when I tell the guys what I've decided—that I only want Lucas tonight, despite my prior amenability to another three-way? Will Lucas feel like I'm reneging on our deal? Will he demand his money back? And, if he does, what the heck will I tell Danica?

With each step I take toward Lucas's door, the more anxious I feel about the situation—and that pisses me off. Why the hell am I becoming a prude all of a sudden? There was a time in my life when I wouldn't have cared where Camden stuck his dick inside me, especially if letting him do it would get Lucas off. So what's my problem now?

I reach the door of the penthouse suite and raise my fist to knock but freeze when I hear Lucas inside. He's singing and playing his guitar behind the door and the sound is absolutely mesmerizing. I don't recognize the song Lucas is playing and can't make out his lyrics, but it's instantly intoxicating. The kind of song you hear blaring out of a passing car and immediately grab your phone to figure out what it was.

Yeah, that settles it. I'm being stupid here. Last night was an amazing, erotic experience. I need to stop overthinking things and go with the flow. If, somehow, another threesome is going to help inspire the genius on the other side of this door to write more songs like this one, then I should throw a haymaker on the angel on my shoulder and let my freaky little devil run the show.

Lucas lets out one final soaring note in his song and the room falls silent.

And that's my cue.

I take a deep breath and rap on the door, my heart throbbing, determined to tell Lucas I'm up for whatever he wants, no matter what it is. But the door to the suite opens, and Lucas, with a massive hard-on bulging behind his jeans, yanks me into the room like he's saving me from a runaway train before I can say a word.

The minute we're both in the suite, Lucas slams the door behind us, pins me against a wall, and, for the first time ever, lays a passionate kiss on me that makes my entire body explode with desire. Oh my God, this kiss! It's everything I've ever fantasized kissing Lucas Ford would be! He's not merely kissing me. He's consuming me. *And I'm absolutely enraptured.*

Lucas pulls out of our kiss, gasping for air. "I told Cam not to come," he says. "I decided I don't want to share."

Every cell in my body is alive with excitement. I'm dying to know why Lucas changed his mind, of course. But that's clearly a conversation for later. "Good," I blurt.

Lucas doesn't hesitate. He rips off my clothes like they're on fire, followed by his jeans and briefs. And in no time flat, he's got one of my hard nipples in his mouth and his fingers stroking between my legs.

As his fingers continue working me into a frenzy, he kisses and nips and licks and sucks his way down my writhing torso until he's on his knees before me. He teases my belly ring with his tongue and laps at the angel tattoo on my pelvic bone for a moment, and then he slides his large hands around me, grabs my ass, and pulls my crotch into his face.

Of course, I'm assuming he's going to immediately devour my bull's-eye, but he doesn't. To the contrary, he shocks the hell out of me by nuzzling my clit with his nose and inhaling deeply, like he's sniffing the bouquet of the finest *pinot noir* from a wine decanter.

"You smell so good," he whispers, his warm breath teasing my clit. "I love your aroma, baby."

I should be embarrassed, right? Self-conscious, perhaps?

But I'm not.

In fact, I'm nothing but turned on.

He nuzzles my clit with his nose and inhales loudly again, and then, finally, blessedly, grips my hips, leans into my crotch, and begins lapping at my bull's-eye with so much fervor, I'm momentarily incapable of breathing.

When I'm able to inhale again, I prop my right thigh onto Lucas's muscled shoulder, tilt my pelvis into his hungry mouth, and ride his beautiful face like I'm trying to smother him.

"I'm addicted," he says between my legs, his voice strained.

I grab Lucas's dark hair to steady myself as he eats me with rhythmic, lapping motions of his tongue and lips, my pelvis matching his mouth's motion. "Lucas," I breathe. "So good."

Without stopping what he's doing with his mouth, he slides his fingers deep inside me and massages my G-spot for mere seconds. And that's all she wrote. A tidal wave of euphoria crashes down on me.

I claw at his bare shoulders, gasping, growling, gripping his hair. I'm a wild animal in heat. Is this pleasure or pain? Because it feels like it's ripping me in two. *And it feels so good.*

Lucas takes my thigh off his shoulder and bolts up to his full height, his dark eyes burning, his lips slick with my juices, and plunges himself inside me, banging me into the wall as he does.

"Angel," he whispers into my ear, his massive cock impaling me. "Assassin." He picks me up by the ass and I wrap my thighs around his waist, my body fucking the hell out of his. "Whoever the fuck you are, you're amazing."

I let out a guttural growl and grab his hair furiously as he fucks me, and he swoops in for a passionate kiss. I suck his lower lip. Moan into his mouth. Oh, fuck, I'm losing my mind.

Another orgasm slams into me. The muscles surrounding Lucas's cock squeeze and ripple fiercely, and he growls and groans along with me.

"Holy fuck, it feels good when you come," he grits out. But somehow, when I'm done with my orgasm he's still hanging on, if only by a thread. "Suck me, baby," he commands.

"Yes, sir."

In one fluid motion, I sink to my knees and take him into my mouth and show him just how much he turns me on.

A few minutes later he blurts, "Oh, Jesus," and comes into my mouth.

I swallow him down eagerly and look up at him from my knees. I feel drunk. Addicted. I'm his to command. Whatever he wants, I want to give it to him.

Lucas looks down at me and smiles. "Come here." He pulls me up, takes me into his arms, and kisses me. "I've never met anyone like you," he whispers.

"Like me?" I ask.

"A woman who gets off like you do. It gets me off. It's so fucking hot."

"It's so fucking abnormal."

"Fuck normal," Lucas says. "Holy mother of God. Camden said you had unbelievable talent, but that was *supernatural*. I can honestly say that was the best blowjob I've ever had."

I bite my lip. "My parents would be so proud."

"Fuck your parents," he says. "That's talent, baby."

I laugh. "So why did you tell Camden not to come tonight? Last night you seemed so gung ho about having another threesome."

"I was," he says. "But then after I talked to you in the lobby I came back up here and wrote this incredible song about you and..." He trails off.

"And...?" I prompt.

He shrugs. "And for some reason when I was done writing that particular song, I felt so..." He sighs. "Let's just say the thought of sharing you with anyone didn't turn me on anymore." He cocks his head. "Are you disappointed?"

"I'm relieved. Elated, actually. I was feeling the exact same way. The more I thought about it, I couldn't figure out where I'd be willing to put Camden's dick."

His face lights up. "Exactly! The more I thought about it, I was like, 'Well, Camden can't have her *ass*. That's mine. And, obviously, he can't have her pussy. Nobody gets her pussy but me. And the bastard's already had the good fortune of getting this purportedly amazing blowjob from her, so now it's my turn to get some of that.'"

I can't help laughing.

He shoots me a boyish smile. "Come on, baby. I'm dying to show you my new song about you." He grabs my hand and leads me toward the couch. "We'll eat a little something, I'll sing to you, and then I'll fuck your brains out again." He chuckles. "That was my plan when I opened the door, actually. I just got a little carried away."

CHAPTER TWENTY-THREE

Lucas calls down for room service and we talk easily for a bit while waiting for the food to arrive. In response to my endless questions, Lucas tells me stories from his various tours and albums, and I laugh and gasp and fawn all over him like the fangirl I am. I ask him about some of his more ambiguous lyrics, and he answers all my questions without a hint of impatience or annoyance. I ask him about his childhood, and he tells me about how he grew up with a single mother who worked as a grocery store clerk right up until "Shattered Hearts" hit number one all over the world.

"When I was growing up," Lucas says, "my mom always used to say, 'One day, Lukie, we're going to live in a house near the beach—so close to the sand, we'll swim in the ocean every day, if we want.' So the minute I got my first big royalty check from 'Shattered Hearts,' I bought my mom a six-bedroom house in Malibu, right on the sand, and I told her, 'Looks like it's time to buy yourself a closetful of bathing suits, Mom. One day is finally here.'" His pride is unmistakable.

My heart is bursting at the look on Lucas's face. "You're close to your mom?" I ask.

"Very."

"Was it your mom who got you into music?"

Lucas nods. "I used to stutter really badly when I was a kid.

It was awful. I had all these amazing thoughts bouncing around in my head, but no way to get them out. I wrote poetry a lot, but that certainly wasn't making me any friends. I became so withdrawn, kids at school started figuring I was just stupid or slow. And after a while, I started thinking it about myself, too. We didn't have money for speech therapy or anything like that, so I didn't really think there was any way out of the darkness for me." He looks deep in thought for a moment. "And then, one day, my mom came home with a second-hand guitar she'd bought off some dude at work, plus a big ol' stack of 'Teach Yourself How to Play Guitar' books. And she said, 'You can say what you need to say this way, Lukie. Let it pour out of you.' And, man, that was it. The minute I touched the strings of that beat-up guitar, it was like everything changed for me. I instantly knew exactly why I was put on this earth."

I'm blown away. I've watched and read countless Lucas Ford interviews over the years and not once have I heard him tell this particular story to anyone. "Wow," I whisper. "I just got chills, Lucas."

He nods solemnly. "I swear I'd be dead by now if it weren't for that first guitar from my mom. She literally saved my life."

I'm dying to ask Lucas a thousand follow-up questions, but a loud knock on the door thwarts my plan.

"Room service!" a clipped voice shouts.

"Shit," I whisper. I pop up and sprint into the bedroom to hide as Lucas gets up to answer the door, chuckling at my reaction.

After the room service guy has left, Lucas and I settle ourselves onto the couch with our plates.

"Enough about me," Lucas says, chomping on a cheeseburger. "Tell me about you."

"I already told you the basics the other night, right after you played 'Assassin' for me, remember?"

"You told me almost nothing the other night," Lucas says.

I shrug. "There's not much to say. If you've got a question, I'll answer it."

Lucas purses his lips. "When did you first discover your motor runs so damned hot?"

"I don't know how to answer that."

He considers. "Okay, how about this... Was there ever a time when you thought, 'Hey, I think I might be way more sexual than other girls'?"

I feel my cheeks blaze. "Yes."

"Tell me about it."

"It's embarrassing."

"Why?"

"Because I'm, you know, abnormal. I'm '*aberrant.*'"

"Who says?"

I bite my lip, not wanting to get into it.

Lucas scoffs. "Whoever said that about you, fuck 'em, Abby. You're not 'aberrant,' you're awesome." He eats a french fry. "But if it makes you feel any better, I'm 'abnormal' and 'aberrant,' too. Whatever you've done, I guarantee you, I've done ten times worse."

I've never talked about my shameful past with anyone but Dr. Carlson, but all of a sudden, looking into Lucas's eyes, I want to unburden myself with him. I test the waters by telling him the story of how, in ninth grade, right after sitting through a sex education class for the first time, it became clear to me the class had affected me differently than it did my friends. "They all thought the class was titillating and exciting, of course," I say, "but after we all talked and giggled for like twenty minutes, my friends were ready to move on to other topics. But me? My brain literally couldn't move on. I hadn't even been kissed at that point yet, but I suddenly felt like a junkie in need of a fix."

"So did you wind up fucking the entire football team at age fourteen, or what?"

"No, having actual sex didn't seem like an option to me at that point. I went to a conservative prep school, and my home life was really restrictive, so it was more that I was overwhelmed with obsessive sexual thoughts. Every man I saw, I imagined him, if only briefly, buck naked with a massive, straining hard-on. I wondered what their faces might look like when they had an orgasm, what noises they'd make when someone was giving them head. When men talked to me, I saw their lips moving but I zoned out on their words because I was too obsessed with the idea of their lips eating a pussy—not necessarily mine, you understand. It was more that I was having an epiphany that everyone in the world was having sex and oral sex all around me."

Lucas chuckles. "I had the exact same epiphany as a teen. Totally normal, Abby."

"No, no, this wasn't within the range of normal. I started watching porn, which was a trick in and of itself, since the computers at my house had child restrictions on them. And once I saw actual women—and men—sucking dicks and getting fucked, and I got to see the looks of rapture on their faces, I was a goner. I started touching myself every night and imagining I was in the pornos I'd watched...all while staring at a certain rock star's face on my wall for inspiration, by the way."

He smiles.

"And then one night," I continue, "out of nowhere, I gave myself my first orgasm—while looking at your face, of course. And that was it. I was addicted."

"And *then* you did the entire football team?"

I laugh. "No. No football players were screwed during the making of this particular porno."

He laughs.

"For me, once I finally started having sex at sixteen, it wasn't about the *quantity* of my conquests, it was about the *quality* of them." I pause and bite my lip. "The 'forbidden fruit' factor was very, very enticing to me." I shrug like I'm done talking.

"Oh, hell no," Lucas says. "Don't stop now, baby. Things are just getting good."

I swallow hard.

"Abby, there's nothing to be embarrassed about. I'm a freak, too. Come on. I'm sure it's no big deal."

I take a deep breath and then just spit it out. "I got a rush from sleeping with unavailable or unattainable men. I liked *conquering* them. Making them obsessed with me and then leaving them to pick up the pieces after I was gone."

He smiles broadly. "*Assassin.*"

I bite my lip.

"So how'd you do it? How'd you make men obsessed with you?" He smiles again like he finds that highly amusing.

"I'm not going to tell you if you're just going to laugh at me."

"I'm not gonna laugh at you. I'm smiling because you surprise me. Because you're awesome."

I take another deep breath. "I just always knew exactly how to do it. Don't ask me how. Whoever the guy was that I wanted, I always knew the special thing that would seduce him. So that's what I did. The rush was making the guy do things he otherwise wouldn't. I liked knowing I'd broken down his good judgment. That I was a drug he couldn't resist."

Lucas's face is on fire now. "Jesus, Abby. You're sexy as hell. What the fuck did you do to those poor men? Did you make 'em rob a bank for you?"

I roll my eyes. "I was never motivated by money. It was all about the forbidden rush for me. Breaking them down and making myself feel powerful." My cheeks flush. "I wanted to feel wanted— *desperately* wanted—if only briefly."

"I take it you didn't get too much of that growing up—feeling wanted?"

I swallow hard again, stuffing down the emotion threatening to rise up inside me. "Not a whole lot."

"Tell me what happened. I won't judge, I promise."

I twist my mouth, considering. "Maybe later. I've got to get back to work and I'm dying to hear your new song."

Lucas considers that for a moment. "Okay, then, fair enough. But we're not done with this conversation. We'll talk about this further tomorrow night."

I nod.

Lucas grabs a box of cigarettes off the coffee table and pulls one out. "Just one quick question, though," he says. "Why'd you ask me for thirteen grand? It's such a weird number. Is that how much you owe on your car or something?"

"It's not for me. This woman I work with—Danica—her mom was in a pretty bad car wreck last year and that's how much she owes in medical bills."

"You're giving your fee to your friend's mom?"

I nod.

"*All* of it?"

I nod again.

"But don't you have a car payment or something?"

"Well, yeah, I've got student loans—loads of them—but I'm so far in the hole, thirteen grand won't even make a dent. I figure it's better to make someone else's life immeasurably better than to make mine point-oh-five percent better."

"How much debt are you in from law school?"

"It doesn't matter. It's insurmountable."

"Fuck, you're annoying. Just answer the question."

"About one fifty. But it's okay. I'll be able to pay it off eventually after I graduate and get a job and work for ten years."

"Shit, law school's expensive. With a price tag like that, I hope you love it."

I look at him like he's nuts.

"You don't love it?"

"I hate it."

"Then why the fuck do you go?"

"Because I don't happen to be a rock star. Now sing me your song before I've got to go back downstairs. I'm sure Danica's freaking out about how long I've been gone."

"I'll throw her another grand for her inconvenience. Just

explain it to me. Why the hell are you going to law school if you hate it so much?"

I throw up my hands, exasperated. "Lucas. *Come on.* Play me your song."

"Tell me why you're going to law school or no song."

I roll my eyes. "My dad is the founding partner of an international corporate law firm and he's made it clear he expects me to work for him. Luckily, the firm's got offices all over the world, including in Manhattan, where I've always dreamed of living, so I figure with my parents living in D.C., I'll still feel like I'm relatively free, even if I work for my father's firm."

Lucas takes a long drag off his cigarette. "Baby, take it from me, there's no such thing as 'relative freedom.' You're either free or you're not."

I flash him a look of pure annoyance. Why the heck is he probing me about all this?

"So lemme see if I accurately understand this cluster fuck you call your life," Lucas says, apparently deciding to disregard the look of annoyance I'm flashing him. "Your father owns a huge-ass law firm with offices all over the world and yet you're in debt up to your eyeballs to go to law school so you can work in a job you don't even want?"

I smash my lips together.

"Abby, do you have any idea how fucked up this is? If your dad's loaded, he should foot the bill for his daughter's education, especially if he expects her to work for him at his swanky law firm. I mean, shit, there should be *some* perks to having a rich daddy. Not that I'd personally know."

"My family doesn't work that way. My parents haven't helped me financially since I graduated from high school. That's why I'm in so much debt. I've been completely on my own for a very long time."

"Well, if that's the case, then even more reason why you should get to do whatever the hell you want. Fuck your father. It's your life, bought and paid for by *you*."

"Lucas, you don't understand."

"Then explain it."

"I've put my parents through hell. This life is my penance."

"Your penance for what? You were young and curious and slightly fucked up. Who'd you fuck? Your daddy?"

I'm aghast. "No! Of course, not!"

"Your daddy's best friend?"

"No! It was nothing like that."

"Then whatever you did, you don't owe them your life. I can't imagine these past ten years of me being on tour I haven't done ten times more shit than you did at your worst and I don't consider myself 'aberrant' or 'abnormal' or owing penance to anyone." He puts down his cigarette, scoots closer to me on the couch, and takes my face in his hands. "Abby, your dad's no different than the cocksuckers at my label. He's holding you hostage. Well, I say, fuck him and the Mercedes he drove in on. It's your life. Set yourself free, baby."

Tears prick my eyes. "I can't. No more than you can."

Lucas looks at me sympathetically for a very long beat. And then he shocks me by leaning in and kissing me gently.

When we disengage from our sweet kiss, I look into his eyes, feeling like I'm about to melt into a puddle.

"Quit school," Lucas whispers. "Do whatever you want with your life. *Please.*"

My cheeks are blazing. My heart is racing. I truly feel like I've just fallen in love. "I just can't," I say weakly, emotion threatening to well up inside me. I swallow hard and stuff it down. "I'm in too deep now. The only way I could possibly earn enough money to pay for all the student loans I've racked up over the years is getting a job at a top-tier law firm like my father's. I figure I'll work at my dad's firm after graduation for however many years to get myself out from under my debt and then, hopefully, one day I'll..."

Lucas strokes my hair. "One day you'll what?"

I shake my head. I've never said this out loud to anyone. It's preposterous, really. Completely ridiculous.

"One day you'll what, Abby?" Lucas asks. "What's your dream for that magical one day in the sky?"

"It doesn't matter." I wipe my eyes and look into his beautiful face. "Just play me your song, Lucas," I say, my voice quavering. "One day doesn't exist for me. It just can't. So please, play me your song and help me forget my fucked-up life for a little while."

He scrutinizes my face. "Abby, I'm contractually obligated to the cocksuckers. I have no choice. But you? You're letting the cocksuckers hold you hostage by choice."

I wipe my eyes again. "Play me the song, Lucas. Please."

He sighs and reaches for his guitar. "I'm not done with you yet, just so you know. I'm going to play the song for you because I'm a weak bastard and I can't resist you when you look at me like that. But trust me, Angel, I'm not even close to being done with you yet."

CHAPTER TWENTY-FOUR

If there's something more mind-blowingly erotic than watching Lucas Ford sitting naked on a couch, passionately performing a song called "Angel" for me, after having just called me Angel, then I don't know what it could be.

The song is the same one Lucas played behind the penthouse door earlier, and now that I'm able to understand the lyrics and watch Lucas's glowing face as he sings it, I'm even more blown away by it. It's utterly brilliant.

The song starts out as whimsical. Kind of funny, actually. Lucas muses about accommodating his angel's rather large feathered wings as he makes love to her. He wonders if she's really an angel, or more like a nymph. *Nymphomaniac*? And then the song takes a decidedly poignant turn. What starts out as Lucas's sexual attraction to his angel turns into something much deeper. He realizes she's maybe not just a vehicle for his pleasure, but perhaps something much more. Perhaps she was *literally* sent from heaven above to free him from his shackles. "Only you can free me, Angel," he croons toward the end of the song. "Free me from myself. Free me from the bloodsuckers and their relentless pursuit of wealth. Angel, let me slide inside you, bring me back to life. Let me get inside you, baby, 'til I feel like I'm not dyin'. Oh, Angel, my sweet Angel, save me with your wings. I've died a thousand deaths to find you, now I'm born again."

When Lucas finishes the song, he opens his eyes and levels me with burning eyes.

I clutch my heart. It feels like it's going to burst out of my chest. "That was amazing."

"I swear it's got to be the best song I've ever written," Lucas says. "And, holy fuck, playing it turns me on." He lifts his guitar to prove it—and I'm met with the delicious sight of his hard penis straining up toward his abs.

"Well, gosh, what a coincidence," I say, grinning. "It just so happens *hearing* that song turns *me* on." I motion with flourish to my crotch, referencing the invisible lady-boner straining up toward my belly, and we both chuckle. "Will the cocksuckers be happy with that song, you think?"

"They already told me they love it."

"Oh, thank God."

"But guess what other thing they said about it?"

I sigh. "It's not the leadoff single?"

"Yup. The cocksuckers want 'Shattered Hearts' two point oh—not a love song—and nothing else will do."

"God, I *hate* them."

Lucas laughs. "Welcome to my world."

"What the heck did you do to those bastards to make them hate you so much? It had to be something horrible."

"I stopped being their puppet. I told them I want to make the kind of music *I* want to make, record sales be damned, and then I went right ahead and wrote an album full of songs I loved." He shakes his head. "And, unfortunately, the album bombed."

I cringe, once again feeling guilty I didn't buy Lucas's third album when it came out.

"You want to hear something crazy?" Lucas says. "Those cocksuckers genuinely think I *wanted* that album to flop. That I wrote it as nothing but a giant 'fuck you' to them, and not from my heart." He scoffs. "So now they hate me with a passion and they don't care one little bit if I stay in artistic purgatory forever."

"But can't you sue them? I'm sure you could claim unfair business practices or breach of the implied covenant of good faith and fair dealing in your contract."

Lucas chuckles. "Look at you, Little Miss Law Student! Ha! Even if you hate law school, I gotta say you're still sexy as hell when you talk like a lawyer, baby."

I smile shyly.

"Well, thanks for the legal advice, counselor," Lucas says. "But after much consideration and consultation with my lawyers, I've come to the conclusion it makes more sense for my life as a whole to just write the fucking song they want and move on. They're cocksuckers, after all, which means they'd fight me hard in court. And I've decided I don't want to be tied up for years in an expensive legal battle when I could just write one last album and be done with it. I just want to make music, you know? That's all I want to do. All I've ever wanted to do."

My eyes lock onto his massive hard-on and, suddenly, I don't want to talk about contracts and legal arguments anymore. I want to get fucked. Without saying another word, I slide to him and straddle his lap, and slowly lower myself onto him.

"Oh my fuck, you feel good," he breathes as his hard-on burrows deep inside me. "How are you so damned wet? I haven't even touched you."

"It was the song," I whisper, my forehead against his. I grab his cheeks and kiss him as I ride him. "That was the sexiest song I've ever heard."

"It was about you," he whispers. "That's why it was sexy."

He grabs my ass and begins leading my pelvis into rhythmic motion on top of him, his eyes fixed on mine, our foreheads pressed together, and all of a sudden a bolt of electricity like nothing I've ever felt before courses between us. I quicken the pace of my movement, sliding my clit against his shaft with each furious snap of my pelvis—and just like that, we're both in a frenzy of pleasure.

"Angel," he whispers. "Assassin. Ass-kicker. Whoever you are, you're *conquering* me. You know that? You're *conquering* me, baby." He grabs my face the way I'm grabbing his and we kiss passionately as our bodies move in synchronicity.

I don't know if he's mocking me by saying I'm conquering him, but I must admit it's turning me on to hear him say it, regardless. I press myself down on his hard-on and attack his mouth, suddenly determined to conquer him in earnest. By God, I'm going to get him to do the one thing he says he never does, the one gift he says he never bestows upon any woman. *I'm going to make this man come inside me.*

"I'm right on the edge," I croak out, my body on the cusp of release. "Come with me," I whisper urgently, grinding down hard onto him, pinning him inside me. "Come with me, Lucas." I inhale sharply and stiffen as a toe-curling orgasm hits me, pressing myself down onto him with all my might, trapping him inside me, forcing him to trust me like no one else. Not three seconds later, Lucas growls, pushes me up forcibly off him...and comes all over my trembling thighs.

CHAPTER TWENTY-FIVE

"You're off from work the next two nights, right?" Lucas asks as he comes out of the bathroom. He grabs his jeans off the floor and begins pulling them on without underwear.

I silently finish clasping my bra and grab my shirt off the floor.

"Abby?"

I pull my shirt on and reach for my skirt.

"Hey," he says. "You okay, Ass-kicker?"

"I'm fine."

"Then why do you look so pissed?"

I fasten my skirt. "I'm not pissed. I'm contemplative."

Lucas sighs. "Abby, I told you. I never come inside a woman. No exceptions."

How the fuckity-fuck did he know what I was scheming to do?

Lucas plops onto the couch and picks up his guitar. "I'm not going to apologize that I don't want to accidentally impregnate you." He begins tuning his guitar. "Sorry, Aberrant Abby. I guess you're just going to have to face the fact that not all guys will let you conquer them."

I clench my jaw. "Don't tease me like that. I didn't tell you about my past so you could mock me about it."

Lucas looks instantly stricken. "I was kidding. Hey, look at me.

I'm sorry. I was just trying—and failing—to make a joke."

I don't reply.

"Abby, I'm an idiot. I'm sorry."

"I'm just really sensitive about that," I say softly. "I've never told anyone the stuff I told you, other than my therapist. I'm not quite at the point where I can laugh about it yet."

"Understood. Won't happen again."

"Thank you."

"So what's your schedule the next two nights?"

"I'm off from work both nights."

"Will you stay here with me both nights?"

"Will you make fun of me again?"

"Yes. But not about the stuff you told me."

I smile. "Okay, then. I'll stay."

"Great."

"I'll have to head out on Saturday morning for my weekly study group, but I'll come right back and stay that night, too."

"Awesome. That's perfect timing, actually. I've got to head off Sunday morning to LA, so this will give us maximum time together before I leave."

My stomach drops into my toes. *He's leaving on Sunday?* Shit! I'm not even close to ready for this fantasy to end.

Lucas begins strumming his guitar. "Cool. Finish your shift and get yourself some sleep, and when you wake up, pack a bag and get your ass back here, ready for two days of me hounding you to tell me everything I want to know about you."

I'm frozen. I suddenly feel panicked, like I'm hurtling toward a brick wall. If he's leaving Sunday, exactly when does he expect me to break his heart?

"Abby?"

I nod, but my stomach is twisting into knots.

"Babe, I'm kidding. You don't have to tell me anything you don't want to."

He's completely misreading me, of course. But obviously I can't tell him what I'm actually thinking, since we promised not to talk about the game or break character.

"Abby?"

I take a deep breath. "Sorry, yeah, that all sounds good. I better get back to work." I kiss him goodbye and beeline to the door, my mind reeling.

"Bye, baby," he says behind me, strumming his guitar. "Come back the minute you wake up this afternoon, okay? I'll be here, writing like a fiend. In fact, there's a song I'm gonna start writing the minute you walk out the door."

I turn around to face him, just before reaching the door. He looks deep in thought as his fingers nimbly play an elaborate riff on his guitar.

Please, God, let whatever song he's working out right now be the one that sets him free so I don't have to do it. "What song are you going to write when I leave?" I ask hopefully, my heart aching. "The second coming of 'Shattered Hearts'?"

"Nope," Lucas says, almost gleefully, his fingers moving masterfully up the frets of his guitar. "I'm not even close to writing that song yet. The next song I write's going to be called 'Aberration.'" He beams a truly lovely smile at me. "And don't worry, Angel, it'll be another love song—not to mention a giant 'fuck you' to your cocksucking parents." He flashes me a mischievous grin. "I promise, sweetheart, you're going to *love* it."

I try to return Lucas's beaming smile, but I can't. "I can't wait to hear it," I manage to choke out, turning my back on him and turning the handle of the door.

"Hey, Abby?"

I turn around and look at him expectantly, hoping he's about to tell me the role-play isn't necessary anymore—that he's decided we're going to hang out together for the next two days with no agenda beyond pure enjoyment.

"Toss me your undies, baby," Lucas says. He winks. "I want to have access to your aroma at all times. All in the name of artistic inspiration, of course."

CHAPTER TWENTY-SIX

The lobby is bathed in golden, pre-sunset light when I enter The Rockford just before seven on Friday evening with an overnight bag in my hand. A guy named Pablo I barely know is currently standing behind the front desk. He looks at me quizzically as I pass by, obviously wondering what the night shift girl is doing here at this time of day and on her day off.

I wave breezily. "Hey, Pablo. I just dropped by to pick up some paperwork before heading off to..."

But I don't need to finish my lie. Pablo's already waved back at me and he's now looking down at his computer again.

Well, that was easy.

I stride to an elevator, step inside, and swipe the key card Lucas gave me to allow access to the penthouse floor. Why do I suddenly feel like I'm walking a gangplank?

The elevator door opens on the penthouse floor and I walk down the hall, breathing deeply to steady my racing heart. Yes, of course, I'm thrilled at the prospect of spending two full nights with Lucas, but even more so I'm feeling nervous about the inevitable crash ending to this fairytale. Will I be able to muster the willpower to do what I promised to do, or will I chicken out? Because, at the moment, I simply can't imagine telling Lucas I want anyone but him, even if we both know it's a lie.

I reach Penthouse A and stand outside the door, and once again I'm bowled over by the sound of music emanating from inside the room. I can tell it's another new song, but I can't make out the words. I lean my ear against the door and strain to decipher Lucas's lyrics, but damn it, I can't make them out. But it doesn't matter. Even without being able to understand precisely what Lucas is singing about, I can *feel* the emotion of the song—and it's absolutely electrifying.

The music inside the suite stops.

And so, I take a deep breath and knock. Ten seconds later, the door opens and Lucas appears, looking as sexy as ever.

This evening, the man who adorned my teenage walls is wearing nothing but black boxer briefs, and he's quite obviously hard as a rock behind them. His dark eyes look wild beyond anything I've seen before. His jaw is covered in stubble. His hair is a disaster. Holy crap, he looks like a madman.

"Lucas," I gasp. Truly, he looks demented. "Have you slept at all since I left?"

I've barely gotten my question out when Lucas yanks me into the suite and begins quite literally ripping my dress off my body.

"Lucas," I breathe, instantly aroused by his urgency.

Lucas flings my dress onto the floor, pulls my G-string off with a loud grunt, unlatches my bra, and before I can say or do a damned thing, he presses his lips to mine, slides his fingers deep inside me, and fondles my breast with his free hand. "What took you so long to get here?" he whispers. He bends down and buries his face in my small breasts, like a kid bingeing on cookies. "I'm *hungry* for you," he growls. He sucks fervently on one of my nipples, making me inhale like I've just touched a hot stove. He gropes my ass. Bites my neck. Strokes my clit. Growls with his arousal. "I've been sitting here with your scent for hours, writing another amazing song about you, driving myself crazy." He fucks me with his fingers, and presses his hard-on against my hip. "It was your *aroma* that did this to me. I haven't written like this in forever. I feel fucking *alive*."

I peel his briefs down and his massive erection springs out, its tip already shiny and wet, and I moan at the beautiful sight of it.

Once his briefs are off and thrown across the room, he scoops me up by my ass, slides me onto his hard-on, and strides toward the bedroom, kissing me furiously as he walks.

"I missed you," I coo, grinding myself onto his hard-on, my excitement ramping up instantly.

"I'm addicted to you," he whispers. "You're my drug." He lays me down on the mattress, spreads my legs like a butterfly, leans in, and inhales deeply. "Oh, baby, that's the drug right there." He skims his stubbled chin against my crotch as he works me with his fingers and inhales my scent again. "I think I'm having some kind of breakdown." He begins licking me, nibbling me, nuzzling me. And when he finally goes in for the kill and penetrates me deeply with his tongue, we both let out loud moans of pleasure together.

When I come for him, he strides to the nightstand, opens a drawer, and pulls out a nylon rope.

My eyes widen. I've actually got a whole bunch of goodies in my overnight bag—handcuffs, a blindfold, a dildo, a tickler—but he doesn't know that. How did he know I'd be up for some kinky fuckery tonight?

"Yes?" he asks, holding up the rope.

"Fuck yes." I arch my back and spread my legs. "*Sir.*"

Lucas smiles wickedly and begins tying my left wrist to the headboard. "I'm going to give you the night of your life, Angel," he whispers, his voice husky. "To thank you for giving me the best songs of mine."

I'm about to hyperventilate from sheer excitement. "My bag," I blurt. "I brought toys."

One side of Lucas's beautiful mouth tilts up. "Of course, you did. Because you're an angel sent straight from heaven." He moves onto tying my other wrist. "Have I ever told you you're perfect, Abby?"

"No."

He licks one of my erect nipples, making me moan. "Well, let me say it now. Abby the Ass-kicker Assassin Angel, you're fucking perfect."

CHAPTER TWENTY-SEVEN

The sound of the radio in the other room slowly pulls me out of my dream. I touch the other side of the mattress, expecting to feel Lucas's naked, warm body next to mine, but he's not there. And, just like that, I realize I'm not in my own bed being awakened by a Lucas Ford song on the radio. I'm in the penthouse suite of The Rockford Hotel and Lucas Ford himself is strumming his guitar and singing softly in the other room. *How is this my life?*

I open my eyes groggily and look at the clock. It's just after four in the morning. God, my internal clock is totally wacked out these days.

For a long moment, I lie on my back, stretch my body out, and think about the filthy and fantastic sex Lucas treated me to earlier. Damn, that was fun. Raw. Primal. *Dirty as hell.* The kind of sex I've always dreamed of having with a boyfriend but haven't been able to achieve because nobody's ever been confident enough to take me as far as I want to go. But Lucas sure did. In fact, he didn't hold back one bit. God, we were totally in synch, the two of us—no boundaries or limits. And it was unbelievably amazing.

To start things off tonight, Lucas and I had a nice little three-way with my vibrating dildo—and *lots* of lube—with Lucas claiming my ass while the dildo filled up my cooch. Holy hell, did I have a monster of a gushing orgasm that time. *Delicious*. Especially when Lucas licked it up like it was whipped cream.

After that—and after Lucas had fastened an itty-bitty vibrating clamp onto my clit—he titty- and face-fucked me like a blow-up doll, demanding I call him "sir" and that I beg him to come all over my breasts—which he kindly did.

But Lucas my master wasn't finished with me yet, even though he'd already given me the night of my life. While his body recharged, he tied me up again, blindfolded me, and proceeded to drive me wild with his lips and tongue and teeth, not to mention my bag full of toys. Holy mother of God, that was divine.

And, finally, the *pièce de résistance...* When my slack body was finally spent and my head lolling to the side from complete sexual exhaustion, Lucas untied me and removed my blindfold and took me tenderly into his arms and kissed me like I was the great love of his life. And then he whispered something into my ear no man but Lucas has ever said to me, but which he keeps saying to me like it's an objective fact. "You're perfect, Abby."

Sweet Baby Jesus, I've never experienced a more blissful moment than that.

The sound of Lucas singing softly in the living room of the suite draws me out of my memories of last night and back to the present moment.

With a huge smile on my face, I stretch myself out on the bed and listen to Lucas singing. He's a musical genius, that man. There's simply no other way to accurately describe him.

I slide off the bed and pad into the darkened living room.

Lucas is sitting on the couch in the moonlight, naked and

playing his guitar, his muscles and tattoos on glorious display. Wow, he looks so damned beautiful right now, I want to drop to my knees and blurt every last thing on my mind to him. I want to tell him he's perfect—my idea of perfect. I want to tell him everything I've done. Who I am. I want to confess I've destroyed lives in the past and that I'm sorry about it. I want to tell him I haven't had a problem in years, but that I'm so damned lonely these days, it's hard to get too excited about measuring "progress" in terms of "the absence of problems."

I want to tell Lucas it sometimes feels like my life is empty. Like I'm headed toward a pointless, joyless oblivion, followed by death. I want to tell him when I'm with him I feel alive in a way I've never felt before. Adored. Loveable. I want to tell him when I'm with him I feel *hopeful*. Like maybe there is a point to all this craziness, after all.

I want to tell Lucas I'm falling head over heels in love with him. For real, and not as part of an "extended role-play."

And, most of all, I want to beg Lucas to take me with him to Los Angeles because I'm pretty sure I'm going to fall apart after he leaves me, despite my best efforts to keep it together.

But of course I don't say any of it. Because I know full well none of it is part of our deal. And because I know this particular man needs to be free a lot more than he needs a doting girlfriend, especially an emotionally damaged one.

I settle myself next to Lucas on the couch and listen to him playing his latest song, my heart panging almost painfully. He's singing about a girl who's become a "supernatural addiction" for him. A girl who somehow knows exactly what to do to "bring him to his knees" and "conquer" him.

As I listen, my stomach drops further and further into my toes.

Damn. If only he hadn't hired his "supernatural addiction" to crush him at the end of this week, it'd be a truly lovely song.

CHAPTER TWENTY-EIGHT

When Lucas finishes singing "Addiction" for me, he smiles at me, his eyes glinting in the dim light of the room. "What do you think?"

"I love it."

"Wait 'til you hear it when I record it with the full band. I've already got the entire arrangement figured out in my head. It's gonna have a bass-heavy beat—an *addicting* beat."

"I can't wait to hear it."

Lucas puts his guitar down. "Come here, baby. You're too far away. My skin aches for you."

I slide onto his lap, nuzzle my nose into his cheek, and inhale his masculine scent. I skim my lips over his and run my hands through his hair, reveling in him. "You're a genius," I whisper. "Mark my words. This is going to be your biggest album yet."

Lucas kisses my lips. "You're the secret sauce."

My heart skips a beat. "I'm not doing anything."

"You're doing more than you know."

"Lucas?"

"What?"

I sigh. "Nothing. Never mind."

He brushes my hair out of my eyes and skims his lips over mine. "You know what?"

"What?"

"I like being here inside this little bubble with you. It's nice taking a break from being 'Lucas Ford' for a while."

"It's nice taking a break from being 'Abby Medford' for a while, too."

Lucas brushes his fingertips down the curve of my neck. "The paparazzi were getting to you, too?"

I chuckle. "Yeah. Damned paparazzi."

Lucas chuckles and touches my hair again. "Who would you be if you could be anyone you wanted?" He strokes the back of my neck, gently massaging my tired muscles. "Would you quit law school?"

I nod.

"And then what would you do? Tell me, baby. Assume you had no student loans and didn't give a fuck what your parents wanted. Who would you be?"

"I'd be a writer living in New York City."

"Wow, you had that answer right on the tip of your tongue."

I nod.

"You wouldn't be a kindergarten teacher?"

I chuckle. "No. Although, standing offer, I'd be happy to read you a bedtime story any time you like."

"Why, thank you." He continues stroking the muscles of my neck. "What kind of writer would you be?"

I close my eyes at his glorious touch. "I'd work for a magazine. Not a fashion magazine, more like an edgy men's magazine. Something like *Maxim*."

"Always full of surprises. What would you write?"

"Articles for men from a female perspective. It'd be sexy stuff about what women really want and how to please them. Insight into what makes women tick. But I'd also write observations about life and sex in general. The same kinds of things I write about in this anonymous blog I write."

He looks surprised. "You write a blog?"

"Just for fun—to blow off steam."

"What's it called?"

"*Penelope Pleasure, Miss Pleasure to You!*"

Lucas chuckles. "Show me."

"Really?"

"Hell yeah."

I slide excitedly off his lap and he grabs his laptop.

I navigate to my blog and he begins to read. To my surprise, he doesn't give my writing a cursory glance. He reads my three most recent entries like he's studying them for an exam. Finally, he looks up from his screen. "Abby, this is great. Well written. Sexy as hell. Your voice is totally original. And holy shit, woman, you're hilarious, too—way more so in writing than in person. No offense."

"I'm deeply offended."

"I can't believe I've been fucking a genius writer this whole time. And here I thought you were just a semi-funny-ish kindergarten teacher. Who knew?"

"Why is it I'm not sure if you're complimenting or insulting me?"

He laughs. "I just mean you're a badass of epic proportions but you don't let down your guard enough to broadcast that. It's like you're hiding Superman underneath Clark Kent. I knew you were smart and funny, but I had no idea you were *this* smart and funny."

Every square inch of my skin is covered in goose bumps. "Thank you," I say softly. "That means so much, coming from a genius like you."

Lucas grabs my face in his large palms, bubbling over with enthusiasm. "Why the fuck do you play your cards so close to your vest when you've got this amazingness bouncing around in your head?" He motions to his laptop. "Why not be *that* girl all the time? Forget conquering men. Let Penelope Pleasure conquer the world."

I scoff. "I can't be Penelope all the time. She's nothing but a fantasy. Abby's got to live in reality and pay her bills and function and not, you know, bring shame to her family. That's why I do the blog anonymously. If my parents ever found out about it they'd disown me."

"So what? You're a grown-ass woman. Fuck 'em. They'll survive."

"It's not that simple, Lucas. I've already put my parents through hell."

"Here we go again. *How* did you put them through hell? You still haven't told me what went down."

I don't reply.

Lucas puts his fingertip underneath my chin. "I guarantee you, whatever you did back then, you're *way* overcompensating for it now."

I remain mute.

"Abby, you're not the same girl you were at seventeen, any more than I'm the same seventeen-year-old dumbfuck who sold his soul to the devil." He strokes my cheek with his thumb. "We live and learn, baby. That's how it works. After a while, we figure out everybody else is imperfect, too, and we forgive ourselves for our sins. Live and fucking learn."

Tears prick my eyes.

"What happened when you were a train wreck?" he coos. "Tell me what happened, baby."

"Which time?"

He smiles. "All the times."

I sigh. "That would take too long. Suffice it to say, if there was a man I couldn't or shouldn't have, he was the one I wanted. And if there was something a man didn't want to do, that's the thing I wanted him to do for me. I could tell you a bunch of stories, but the two biggies were that I gave my AP English teacher a blowjob in his classroom during my senior year of high school, not realizing there was a security camera capturing the whole thing. And then I followed up that fiasco a year later by having an affair with my Art History professor at Brown. It turned out he was married with a newborn baby—facts I unfortunately only discovered a month into our illicit relationship. His wife found out about us and shamed me all over social media—a lovely experience that led me to get the hell out of Brown and transfer to the University of Denver just to get away from all the gossip and scandal. And so, here I am. I came to Denver to start a new life—plus a whole lot of therapy—and I wound up staying for law school."

"How long ago was that thing with the professor in college?"

"Five years."

"And you haven't had what you'd consider a problem since?"

"Nope. I mean, don't get me wrong, when I first moved here, I continued making horrible choices in men for about two years. I kept choosing losers and 'bad boys' who were all too happy to have a girl like me in their bed but not in their life. But it was pretty standard she's-got-no-self-respect kind of stuff. No scandals or major issues for the past five years. Actually, for the past two years—ever since I started law school—I've been so squeaky clean and 'healthy,' I'm practically a born-again virgin. All my dirty thoughts get aired in my blog and nowhere else, and certainly not acted upon."

Lucas shakes his head sympathetically. "Come here," he whispers. He wraps his arms around me and kisses me, and soon he's got me on my back on the couch and he's on top of me, entering me, moving inside me, kissing me, whispering into my ear that I'm beautiful and perfect and fuck my parents and fuck trying to be anyone I'm not.

I grab his face and kiss him passionately, emotion welling up inside me. "I've been so ashamed of myself for so long," I whisper, barely able to keep myself from crying. "They said I was 'aberrant.' They said I was 'abnormal.' That nice girls don't have the kinds of urges I do."

"Fuck 'em," he whispers. "You're awesome."

"I've made so many mistakes," I say.

"Live and learn, baby," he says softly, his heart pressed against mine as he moves inside me. "One day you'll figure out how to be you out there in the real world and not just with me. And that's when you'll conquer the world."

The movement of his body inside mine is sending me to heaven. I know we're not supposed to break character or talk about the role-play, but I've got to tell him I can't bear the thought of rejecting him. That I'm falling in love with him and don't want to be without him when this is all over.

"Lucas," I whisper. "Please."

But before I can utter another word, Lucas slams his hips into me, penetrating me as deeply as a man can go. He kisses my mouth with breathtaking fervor, and much to my shock, comes like a bullet train inside me.

CHAPTER TWENTY-NINE

Lucas is chuckling between my legs as he eats me out. It's actually quite strange, to be honest. What's so damned funny? A bit more laughter and my brain suddenly clicks into consciousness. *Oh, I'm dreaming.* I open my eyes to find Lucas sitting next to me in the fluffy bed, laughing his gorgeous ass off while staring at his laptop.

I look at the clock. 6:34 a.m. "What are you laughing at?" I ask.

"Sorry to wake you. I've been reading all your blog posts, starting from the very beginning, and they're hilarious."

I snuggle up to him, lay my cheek on his broad chest, and peek at the screen as he continues to read, my heart soaring.

"I feel like I know you inside and out now," he says. "You really let it all hang out here, don't you? You're fearless."

"*Penelope's* fearless. Abby's a coward."

"Then be Penelope. She's a rock star."

I look up at him, smiling at his word choice, and he kisses my forehead like it's the most natural thing in the world to do.

"Speaking of fearless rock stars," I say. "I downloaded your third album the other day. Talk about fearless. Wow. I'm sorry I didn't buy it when it came out. I feel like an idiot."

"You weren't the only idiot who stayed away from that one, believe me. So did you like it?"

"I loved it. It's a masterpiece. I loved the simplicity of it. No bells and whistles, just honest songwriting. Just your glorious voice."

"Yeah, that's what made it so painful when it bombed," he says. "I put my naked self out there and nobody gave a fuck. All they want is 'Shattered Hearts.' That third album flopping is what made the cocksuckers rein me in and demand I start writing the kinds of songs 'that got me here in the first place' for my fourth and final album."

"I watched the infamous clip from your concert here in Denver," I say. "You wanted to play another song off your third album when your fans started revolting, didn't you?"

"Yeah. I had a little tantrum that night."

"Which song?"

"It doesn't matter."

"It matters to me."

He shrugs. "'Piece of Me.'"

"I really love that one."

"Thanks."

"Are you really never going to sing 'Shattered Hearts' again, like you said that night?"

"I don't know. That's how I feel right now, but I guess I'll see how I feel with a little more time."

I bite my tongue.

"What?" he asks after a long silence.

"Nothing."

"Oh, for the love of fuck. I just read every blog post you've ever written, *Penelope*, which means I'm now well aware you've got strident opinions on everything from lady bugs to butt plugs."

I laugh. "Yeah, but I have no right to have an opinion about this. It's your art."

"Give me your opinion. It doesn't mean I'll be persuaded to change a damn thing I'm doing. I just want to know what you honestly think."

"You sure?"

"Positive."

I take a deep breath. "I think you're seeing this wrong. Yes, 'Shattered Hearts' started out as your song, but it belongs to the world now. Sure, you've played it a million times and have moved on from it, but someone going to one of your concerts is maybe getting to see you perform it for the first time. Maybe some guy in the audience bought tickets to your show for his girlfriend because you're her all-time favorite. Maybe he works a job he hates, but he does it partly because it means he can afford doing fun things like taking his girl to a Lucas Ford concert."

I pause, worried I've overstepped my bounds, but Lucas doesn't seem at all pissed, so I continue. "That song is the soundtrack to your fans' lives. They've lost their virginity to it. Cried to it. *Grieved* to it. You've eased their pain by sharing yours." I shrug. "So I think you should decide to stop feeling like the song is *trapping* you and realize it's a gift. Embrace it. If you feel like you've outgrown playing that song, *as is,* then, okay, you're a musical genius—reinvent it when you play it live. But most of all, be grateful for the gift of so many people loving and feeling moved by your creation. The way I see it, it's the least you can do for getting to do what you love for a living. So few people on this earth get to do that."

There's a moment of stillness between us, during which, I presume, Lucas is deciding whether to physically kick me out of the bed or simply tell me to fuck off.

Lucas abruptly closes his laptop and sets it aside and I hold my breath, waiting for his fury. But that's not what I get. To the contrary, without a word, Lucas pulls me on top of him, slides himself inside me, pulls my face to his, and kisses the living hell out of me. "Ass-kicker," he breathes. *"Thank you."*

CHAPTER THIRTY

I slip out of bed in the late morning light and quietly dress myself, taking great care not to wake Lucas. He's sprawled on the bed, on top of the covers, naked and gorgeous, his breathing rhythmic and slow. Of course, I want nothing more than to skip my study group and stay in bed next to him—and maybe rouse him from his slumber by licking his balls—but the task at hand is looming too heavy on my shoulders to lie here and pretend the sky isn't falling anymore. I've got a job to do here. A wicked, hideous job he's paid me thousands of dollars to do, and I know in my bones I've got to physically leave this suite to detox from our fantasy for a bit if I'm ever going to be able to muster the resolve to do it. Plus, if I'm being honest, a small part of me hopes when Lucas wakes up and finds me gone, he'll miss me, which in turn might prompt him to say, "To hell with the role-play! I want you to come to LA with me, Abby!"

Either way, I'm bone certain I've got to get out of this place for a few hours or I'm going to lose my mind.

I grab my purse off the dresser and begin tiptoeing out of the bedroom.

"Abby," Lucas whispers groggily behind my back.

I jump in surprise and he chuckles at my almost cartoon-like reaction.

"Jesus, you scared me," I breathe. "I thought you were dead asleep."

"Where are you going?"

"Study group."

"Oh, yeah. I forgot about that." He looks crestfallen—which, I must admit, makes my heart flutter with excitement.

Tell me to stay, Lucas. Tell me you don't care about the role-play anymore.

"How soon can you come back?" he asks.

"Later this afternoon. We usually study for a couple hours and then grab lunch."

Please tell me to stay, Lucas.

"Okay. Hey, before I forget..." He indicates the nightstand. "Top drawer."

My stomach drops into my toes. Crap. If Lucas is referring to what I think he is, it's the last thing in the world I want right now.

"Take it now so you don't forget later," he says breezily.

I nod curtly, cross the room on wobbly legs, and open the top drawer. Sure enough, I see an envelope with "Assassin" scrawled across it. I grab the envelope and peek inside and my fears are confirmed. It's filled with hundred-dollar bills.

"I've decided to rip up the NDA," Lucas says softly. "I've thought about it and I think Penelope Pleasure should be free to write about whatever she wants, including 'My Wild Week with Lucas Ford.'"

I'm shocked and I'm sure my face shows it.

"Write about this week, Abby," he says evenly. "Write about it in all its depraved, juicy glory and shop it to whatever magazines in New York you want to write for the most—*Maxim, GQ, Playboy, Esquire,* whatever. A salacious story like that will land you any magazine job you want. Or, fuck it, shop the story to the sleaziest tabloids and get yourself a huge payday. If you work it right, I'm sure you could get a bidding war started. And that ought to get you enough cash at the end of the day to wipe out your student loans and then some. Maybe even get yourself six months' rent on a place in New York on top of clearing your loans."

I'm flabbergasted. He truly thinks I'd tell the world about our time together...for a payday?

"Fair warning, I'll pretend to be pissed about the story," Lucas continues. "But only because if the world thinks I'm raging mad, that'll make the tabloids pay twice as much for it."

I stuff the envelope into my bag, incapable of speaking.

"Hurry back, okay?" Lucas says. "I'm already aching for another hit of my pretty little addiction." His face lights up. "Oh, that's a catchy internal rhyme for the chorus of 'Addiction'—'prit-ty-lit-tle-ad-*dic*-tion.' That's way better than the lyric I've got there now. Shit. Hand me my phone, babe, would you? I want to make myself a note."

I toss him his phone. "Are you going to write another song while I'm out?"

"Maybe even two. I can't keep up with all the ideas slamming into me. They just keep coming and coming."

"Are you going to write the next 'Shattered Hearts' while I'm gone?" I ask hopefully. Please, God, let him say yes and give me a reason to strip off my clothes and crawl into bed and forget the stupid role-play, once and for all.

"Sorry," Lucas replies. "I couldn't write a tortured song like that right now if my life depended on it. The only songs I've got pouring out of me are love songs, thanks to you." He smiles and his eyes sparkle. "Happy people write happy songs, I guess... And miserable people make art."

CHAPTER THIRTY-ONE

I rub my forehead as the members of my study group chat animatedly around me.

I can't concentrate.

All I can think about is the conversation I had with Lucas back in the penthouse...and the envelope full of hundred-dollar bills he made sure I took before leaving. Clearly, he paid me the money before I left to make it clear the role-play's still in full effect. And to ensure I don't chicken out on doing the dastardly thing I agreed to do. And even though I understand he's merely expecting me to follow through on what I promised to do for him, I can't help feeling like he's kicked me in the teeth.

Oh, God, this entire week has been such a mind-fuck. My feelings for Lucas have felt so damned *real*. The conversations we've had, the way we fit together sexually, the songs he's written about me. I'd swear on a stack of bibles we're both feeling the same very real and very intense thing.

And yet...

He paid me. Which means that no matter what he may or may not be feeling for me, or how real or make-believe it may be, he wants me to follow through on my promise, regardless.

Clearly, Lucas wants to be free more than he wants a girlfriend.

And that means that, even though I love him, I've got to honor my promise to him and set him free.

Or... Wait. Perhaps I'm thinking about this all wrong. Maybe I've got to honor my promise to Lucas precisely *because* I love him. *If you love someone, set them free.*

I put my hands over my face, trying not to cry. Yes. That's it. I love him...and that means I've got to do this for him, no matter the pain it will cause myself.

"Abby?" a study-buddy sitting next to me says. "You okay?"

I rub my eyes, stand, and scoop up my laptop and books. "I'm not feeling very well all of a sudden. I think I'd better get some rest."

I say my goodbyes and barrel out of the library toward my car in the parking lot.

If you love someone, set them free.

I reach my car, stumble inside, and sit for a long moment, my fingers wrapped around my steering wheel, tears threatening. If I go back to The Rockford and see Lucas's beautiful face again, I'll lose my resolve. I know I will. I'll throw myself into his arms and beg him to take me with him to Los Angeles. I'll tell him I love him and can't live without him.

And none of that is what he wants or needs.

With a trembling hand, I pick up my phone to call Lucas, and suddenly realize we've never exchanged phone numbers. "Oh, for the love of fuck," I mutter. With a sigh, I press the button to call The Rockford's front desk.

A male voice answers. "The Rockford Hotel. How may I assist you?"

"Is this Theo or Pablo? It's Abby Medford. I work the night

shift."

"Oh, yeah. Hi, Abby. It's Theo."

"Hey, Theo. How are you?"

"Good. What's up?"

"Could you please patch me through to 'Mr. Knobhopper' in Penthouse A? I know he's a restricted-access VIP guest, but I delivered some food to him the other day when he happened to be in the middle of writing an amazing new song, and he was so excited about it he played it for me. Anyway, I gushed about the song, of course, so he told me to come back again today on my day off to hear his next few songs, too—and I just wanted to talk to him briefly to ask if now would be a good time for me to drop by. Obviously, I don't want to bother him if he's busy, and I know he's flagged for no outside calls, but I don't want to be rude and not show up if he was serious about me coming today." I hold my breath and wait, not sure if Theo's a big-picture kind of guy or a slave-to-the-rules kind of guy.

"Wow, lucky you," Theo says.

"Yeah, I know. Right place, right time, huh? He seemed really sincere when he told me to come see him again today. He made me promise twice."

"Okay, yeah, sure, I'll put you through. We wouldn't want him feeling like you ignored his explicit request."

"*Exactly*. Thanks so much, Theo."

The line rings. And rings.

"Yeah?" Lucas finally says brusquely, much to my relief.

"It's me," I choke out.

Lucas's voice turns instantly warm and affectionate. "Hey, angel face," he says softly, and I can hear his sexy smile across the phone line. "I'm aching for you, baby. Get your hot ass back here before I explode."

My stomach tightens. I lean my forehead on my steering wheel, close my eyes, and exhale. "I'm calling to tell you I'm not coming back. I'm calling to say goodbye."

"What? No, not yet, Abby. We've got one more night."

"Goodbye, Lucas."

"Abby, wait. We've got one more night before you do this. I was looking forward to it. *Counting* on it."

"I'm sorry."

"Abby, *wait*. I'm serious. Don't hang up. I'm not heading to LA for another twenty-four hours and I want to spend every one of those hours with you."

"I don't want to be with you anymore." I blink and the tears pooling in my eyes streak down my cheeks. "This is goodbye."

Lucas sounds genuinely distressed. "But you said you'd come back. *I was counting on you coming back, Abby*. What happened?"

"I've got to go now. I'm sorry."

"Stop! *Wait*. Tell me what happened. Whatever it is, we can fix it."

I swallow hard. "I'm sorry, but I've realized I still love Camden."

Lucas exhales audibly like he's greatly relieved. And then he snorts like I've said something absolutely hilarious. "Oh my fuck. For a second there, I thought there was something genuinely wrong." He chuckles. "Baby, we've got another twenty-four hours before I have to leave. That shit can wait. Just come back to me. I'm physically aching for you—like a junkie needing a fix. Let's dive into your bag of toys again. I'm addicted to you."

I squeeze my eyes tight and grip the phone against my ear with white knuckles. "I...I want Camden, not you. I'm sorry."

I can hear him roll his eyes over the phone line. "Okay, press pause on that shit, okay? I want another night with you. I'm going crazy over here. My entire body's aching like I'm in withdrawals. Come back right now. That's an order."

I take a trembling breath. "Goodbye, Lucas," I squeak out, tears streaking down my cheeks.

His voice sounds panicked now. "Abby, time out on the game, okay? Seriously. This is real. I didn't get to kiss you goodbye. I wasn't thinking that was going to be the last time I was going to see you. Now stop fucking around and come back. I mean it."

Tears are streaming from my eyes. "Leave my bag at the front desk when you check out, okay? I know you're going to do great things and I can't wait to see it. But I don't love you and I have to end this now."

"Abby. Wait. Please, I—"

I hang up the call.

"Free yourself, Lucas," I whisper into the silence of my car. I toss my phone onto the passenger seat and stare out my windshield for a long moment. And then I lean forward, place my forehead against my steering wheel, and burst into tears.

CHAPTER THIRTY-TWO

"Sorry I'm late," I say, slipping behind the front desk. "Car trouble."

"No worries," Danica says. She holds up a sealed FedEx envelope. "Pablo said this came for you today."

I grab the envelope from Danica and examine it, my heart thudding in my ears. It's been two weeks since I said goodbye to Lucas during that awful phone call and I haven't heard from him since. Could this possibly be from him?

I inspect the envelope. It's addressed to my attention at the hotel and marked "Personal and Confidential"—and the sender is identified "LDF Enterprises, LLC," with a PO Box address in Los Angeles, California.

"Is Lucas Ford's middle initial 'D,' by any chance?" Danica asks, her eyebrows raised.

I stuff the envelope into my bag, my stomach knotted. "I have no idea."

"Only one way to find out," Danica says.

"I'll open it when I get home. If it's from Lucas, it's probably just a thank you note or thank you tickets to a concert. He said I inspired a whole bunch of songs when he stayed here."

"You're seriously not going to rip that sucker open?" Danica asks incredulously.

"When I get home."

Danica scowls. "Come on, Abby. I'm dying to know what's inside."

"If I open it now, no matter what it is, I won't be able to concentrate on anything else for the rest of my shift. I'll open it later, when I'm home."

Danica rolls her eyes. "You've got ice in your veins, Abigail Medford. I wouldn't last thirty seconds with that thing in my hot little hand."

"More like an emotional self-preservationist," I mutter.

For the next three hours, Danica and I work pretty much nonstop, checking in guests and handling myriad tasks. And believe it or not, I hardly think of Lucas or the envelope at all—*that's a lie*—and when The Dead Zone arrives, I continue *not* thinking about Lucas or the envelope, but instead focus excitedly on my textbook, eager to learn about the seminal Supreme Court case under American antitrust laws.

But when the unmistakable sound of Lucas Ford's haunting voice singing "Shattered Hearts" fills the air, I simply can't resist jerking my head up from my book to discover the source of the sound.

It's Danica, of course. She's staring at her phone at the other end of the check-in counter and Lucas's beautiful voice is wafting out of her hand.

"What are you watching?" I ask.

"A clip of Lucas Ford at his concert in LA last week. It's gone totally viral. He sang a stripped-down version of 'Shattered Hearts.' Just him sitting on a stool with his acoustic guitar, and it's freaking amazing. All the comments say it's even better than the original version with the full band."

My knees wobble.

Damn.

Since my heartbreaking phone call with Lucas two weeks ago, I've promised myself I'm going to avoid hearing Lucas's voice for a full year, just to give my poor shattered heart ample time to mend. But now that this junkie's hearing her drug—and it sounds more gorgeous than ever—I simply can't resist taking a quick hit.

"Play it from the beginning," I say, scooting down to Danica's end of the counter.

Danica squeals and resets the video and we both watch, clutching our chests and oohing and aahing the whole time, as Lucas performs his signature song in a whole new, passionate way.

Lucas finishes his song and the crowd goes absolutely ballistic.

"You liked that?" Lucas asks the large arena, a boyish smile on his face. The crowd responds with a roar of approval.

"Thanks, guys," Lucas says, and he sounds incredibly earnest. A lock of his dark hair falls into his face and he pushes it back. "So, hey, can you guys do me a favor and keep those phones recording for a minute? I want to say something important to you here tonight, but also to everyone out there in Snapchat-opia." He takes a deep breath. "I want to tell you I'm sorry. Lately, I've been a real dick about singing 'Shattered Hearts' for you at my shows, and I owe you a sincere apology for that. I've realized that song isn't mine anymore. It's yours. Nowadays, I'm just the lucky guy who gets to play it for you."

The crowd goes absolutely insane.

Lucas lays his palm onto his muscular chest, right over his heart. "You guys mean everything to me. I promise not to take you for granted ever again. I feel really fortunate to have written a song that's meant so much to so many people for so long. Thank you for being patient with me as I fuck up and stumble and try to figure my shit out. Sometimes, I'm an idiot, guys." He chuckles. "But live and learn, right? That's all we can do in this life."

More enthusiastic applause.

Lucas pauses, seemingly stuffing down acute emotion, and tears prick my eyes at the sight of his obvious vulnerability. Lucas takes a deep breath and gathers himself. "I have a huge announcement for you. Are those phones still recording out there?"

The person behind the device recording whoops along with everyone else in the arena.

"Cool, because I've got great news. I've been writing a ton of new songs lately, and I've finally got everything I need for my fourth album! I'm going to be heading into the studio with the band next month to get started, so I'm guessing you'll have the album in your hands in about a year."

The crowd erupts with unadulterated glee.

"And if you love 'Shattered Hearts,' trust me, you're going to *love* my fourth album. I honestly believe it's going to be my best one yet."

The crowd goes batshit crazy, yet again.

Lucas grins like a little kid. "Okay, enough plugging the new album. Let's get back to the songs you already know and love." He turns back to his band and signals them and then turns to the crowd again, a charming smile on his face. "Let's have some fun!"

Much to the thrill of the arena, Lucas and his band launch into the instantly recognizable introductory riff of his massive hit, "Eat Me Alive," and the clip abruptly ends.

"Wow," Danica says. "Who the hell was *that* guy?"

I open my mouth to reply but quickly realize I won't be able to speak without crying.

"I wonder if some of the songs he wrote here at The Rockford will be on his new album?" Danica says breezily, apparently experiencing no emotional turmoil whatsoever as a result of the video.

But since I can't speak without losing it, I drift back to my open textbook and pretend to study it, willing myself not to let the hurricane of emotion swirling inside me seep out.

Danica chuckles at the other end of the counter. "What a difference from the asshole we met a few weeks ago, huh? Hey, did you ever see a clip of his meltdown at his show here in Denver? Holy hell, it's like he was a different dude from the one in LA. Lemme find it for you." She begins swiping furiously on her phone. "You've got to see this. It's night and day from what we just saw."

"I've seen it," I manage to choke out, my eyes stinging. I clear my throat. "Excuse me."

I stride across the lobby toward the restrooms on rubbery legs, my lower lip trembling, my heart about to burst. Once inside the safety of a stall, I lock the door, sit on the toilet, and let my tears flow.

CHAPTER THIRTY-THREE

After a full shift at work and two classes at school, I haul my exhausted body into my apartment, toss my backpack onto the couch and the unopened FedEx envelope onto the counter, and set about making myself a sandwich in my small kitchen.

Of course, in my wildest fantasies, the envelope contains a one-way plane ticket to LA along with a note from Lucas that says, "These past two weeks, I've realized I'm lost without you, Abby!" But since life isn't a fantasy—and, in fact, doles out knuckle sandwiches quite frequently—I'm guessing there's a better chance pigs will fly than Lucas Ford sending me a declaration of undying love via FedEx. Which is precisely why I've been asking myself a certain question all day long on a running loop as that sealed envelope has burned a hole in my backpack. What, if anything, could possibly be inside that envelope that would make me *almost* as happy as a declaration of undying love from Lucas? And, unfortunately, the only answer I've been able to come up with is *absolutely nothing*.

Let's say, for instance, Lucas feels like we have unfinished business, thanks to that goodbye kiss I denied him, and, therefore, the envelope contains a roundtrip plane ticket to LA and an invitation for me to visit him for a booty call. Would that scenario make me *almost* as happy as a happily ever after? No. Not even close. As much as the instant gratification side of my brain loves the idea of getting to have sex with Lucas again, the mature and rational side of it—*yes, Mom, it seems I really do have one*—knows without a doubt any kind of fuck-buddy situation with Lucas, no matter how thrilling in the short-term, would leave my poor, splintered heart much worse off. So, thanks, but no thanks. I'd rather not subject myself to the eventual agony.

And that's the misery that awaits me if the envelope contains the fuck-buddy invitation I'm predicting it does. What if it shockingly contains nothing more than a pair of concert tickets and a thank you note from Lucas that says something like, "Thank you for being my muse for those awesome days in Miami!"—but Miami is scratched out, and replaced with—"*Denver*! Fondly, Luke." Or, Jesus, what if even *that's* too much to hope for and the envelope actually contains a note from Lucas's "people" that says, "Thank you for being such a devoted fan!" plus a mass-signed photo of Lucas. Gah. It's the possibility the envelope contains something as impersonal as that that's kept me from opening it all morning long.

I finish making my food, staring at the harbinger of my doom on my counter the whole time, and finally head to the couch with my plate and laptop.

Once I'm settled on the couch, I quickly navigate to YouTube and click on various videos posted by audience members of Lucas's LA concert last week. From what I can see from all the different videos, Lucas seems to have performed every single one of his biggest hits that night—which he's not normally known to do. And even more surprising than that, it's quite obvious to me Lucas was having an absolute blast that night performing those hits.

I close my laptop, my body electrified. There's no doubt about it. Lucas is a new man. *He's free.* And that makes me ecstatic for him. I'm way, way happier for him, I suddenly realize, than I am sad for myself.

All of a sudden, the weight of the world has lifted off me. Lucas isn't *mine.* He belongs to the world. And, damn it, the world needs more amazing Lucas Ford songs! When you look at it like that, it's far more important for Lucas to feel inspired to make music than for him to have me as a doting girlfriend. In fact, when you look at it like that, I'm acting like a downright fool.

In a sudden burst of resolve, I place my half-eaten plate of food on my coffee table and leap up to grab the envelope off the counter. Whatever Lucas—or his people—sent me via FedEx, I'll survive my disappointment and eventually move on. I know I will. I got to live an amazing fairytale with Lucas for a few glorious days. I'll hold that inside my heart and treasure it forever. But now it's time for me to accept the fairytale simply doesn't have a happily ever after. At least not for me.

I sit back down on my couch, open the envelope, and reach my trembling hand inside. When I pull it out I'm holding a fistful of confetti scraps covered in tiny print. I look closer and realize the shards of paper are the shredded remnants of Lucas's non-disclosure agreement.

"Oh, Lucas," I whisper.

I reach into the envelope again and pull out a folded notecard—and when I open it a folded square of paper flutters out onto my lap. Oh my God, my heart is exploding.

I read the handwriting inside the notecard.

My beautiful, perfect Angel,

I'll never forget you. How could I? You're the unforgettable Ass-kicker Assassin who didn't take my shit, even though I'm Lucas Fucking Ford (!).

He makes a cute smiley face after that last line.

Thank you for freeing me, Abby. Now free yourself. Write something the world will devour, something that will make all your dreams come true. You deserve to be happy, however you can get there, even if that means Penelope tells the world what a twisted fuck I truly am. I hope our paths cross again one day in NYC, I truly do. But only if you're a writer, making your dreams come true. I wish you the best, always and forever.

Luke

I read Lucas's note ten times, not sure if I want to laugh or cry. Would it have killed him to sign off with "Love, Luke"? Or "XO, Luke," at least? He'll never forget me...and yet he doesn't love me. Not even in some nebulous sort of "love you forever, babe!" kind of way? Well, fuck me.

With a dejected sigh, I pick up the folded square of paper in my lap. "Holy shit!" I blurt the second I unfold it. It's a check made out to me from the account of LDF Enterprises, LLC, for—*holy shit*—two hundred fifty thousand dollars!

I blink my eyes in rapid succession about a hundred times, disbelieving what they're telling me, but the zeros on the check remain unchanged. Holy shit! I have to call Lucas to thank him. I have to tell him this is way too much money. That I didn't do what I did for payment.

I need to tell him I did what I did for *him*. Because—call me a crazy fan, mentally unhinged, a delusional fool, or diehard believer in fairytales—but, honestly, I love him! I do! I have to tell him all these things and more...

Except...

I suddenly remember I can't call Lucas because I don't have his phone number. And, of course, he didn't include it in his note... *because he doesn't want me to call him.*

I rub my forehead. Okay, now I feel slightly mind-fucked, I must admit. The guy gives me two hundred fifty thousand dollars and says he hopes to see me one day, but provides me no means of contacting him to thank him? Does that mean he's planning to contact me one day? And if so, when? Or does it simply mean he's letting me down easy. That Lucas Ford *the artist* is grateful to me for being his muse to the tune of a quarter-million bucks, but Lucas Ford *the man* is quite comfortable letting fate take the wheel on whether or not our paths will ever cross again?

"Shit," I whisper to my empty living room, the reality of the situation dawning on me. *It's Door Number Two.* I know it is. The man I'd give anything to be with doesn't want to be with me. The man gave me a proverbial fishing rod and told me to get out there and catch myself a basketful of fish, and added that if I'm successful he'll perhaps see me on the flip side. One day. Maybe. In New York City. He hopes. But maybe not.

Wow. This is amazing and horrible all at once. I love him and he doesn't love me. But he thinks I might be worthy of his love...one day. Maybe. And he cares enough about me to help me make myself worthy of him. Maybe.

Crap.

So this is what unrequited love feels like, huh? No wonder there are so many songs written about it. It's torture.

I'm suddenly overwhelmed with a tidal wave of gratitude, rejection, hope, despair, heartache, excitement, and most of all, *love* for a generous, talented, and sexy man who cared enough about me to send me a most unbelievable gift. I can't seem to hold myself upright anymore...so I flop forward onto my couch like the victim of a sniper, smash my face into a pillow, and lose myself to sobs.

CHAPTER THIRTY-FOUR

Nine months later...

I raise my arm to hail a cab. I suppose I could walk or take the subway uptown, but I want to be able to sit calmly and look at my notes before I have to do this once-in-a-lifetime, nerve-racking interview mere moments from now. Holy hell, I've never interviewed anyone in my life, let alone the star of one of Hollywood's biggest action franchises! And now I'm supposed to do this without throwing up? How is this my life?

A yellow cab slows down and stops in front of me and I slide into its backseat, shivering from the cold. "Thanks," I say to the driver. "Getting chilly out here." I give the driver the address where I'm headed—a swanky hotel near Central Park—and he nods and pulls back into traffic.

A block into our journey, the new Justin Timberlake song comes on the radio and the driver turns up the volume.

"Oh, I love Justin," he mutters.

"Me, too," I agree.

And that's it for conversation, thankfully.

I pull out my notes for the interview and think about what I'm planning to ask Mr. Movie Star, trying to quiet the voice inside my head that keeps shrieking, "You're in over your head, Medford! Call your boss and tell him to get someone else!"

Thankfully, Brandon Hanover knows I'm a total newbie who's never conducted an actual interview in her life, let alone an interview of a movie star, so that takes the pressure off somewhat. But still, even so, I want to do a great job for my boss. And myself. At a minimum, I certainly don't want to embarrass myself.

It's mind-blowing to me how this opportunity came my way in the first place. According to my boss—whom I've worked with for only three months but already consider one of my all-time favorite people—Mr. Movie Star Brandon Hanover mentioned to him at a press junket that *Maxim* is his favorite magazine and that he happened to catch, and absolutely love, Penelope Pleasure's debut article about sex clubs in the latest issue.

Of course, I was *dying* to think one of the biggest movie stars in the world had read something I'd written, let alone loved it, so I freaked out and maniacally begged to hear every last detail about their conversation, which my boss so generously supplied.

"I loved that sex club article," Brandon Hanover apparently said to my boss. "I popped a boner and laughed—a great combination. Who is this 'Penelope Pleasure'?"

"A blogger who submitted a spec article to us a few months ago," my boss told him.

"Is she a dominatrix or something?" Mr. Movie Star asked.

"If she is, she sure hides it well," my boss reportedly said. "She comes off as super sweet and squeaky clean. She kind of reminds me of Emma Stone."

My boss told me Mr. Movie Star seemed highly intrigued at that point and started asking him a battery of questions about me, all of which ultimately led to my boss explaining I'd been hired by *Maxim* as a freelancer at that point, but that I'd made it clear I was gunning for a permanent position on the writing staff.

"I vote you hire the kid," Mr. Movie Star apparently said. "Make her big dreams come true."

"I would if I could," my boss said he replied. "But the decision isn't all mine. She really needs to make a huge splash with her next article to get the powers that be to take notice of her." And my boss told me that's when he had a brilliant idea. "You know, Brandon," my boss said. "I bet if Penelope landed an interview with one of the world's biggest movie stars, the powers that be would snatch her right up."

And what did that saint of a movie star apparently say in reply to my boss's obvious set up? "Schedule an interview for next week. I'll give her something really good to print."

And now, here I am, six months after moving to New York and three months after landing my first professional writing assignment, on my way to conduct an interview of one of the world's biggest movie stars. *And I'm crapping my pants.* Or, more accurately, my beautiful new designer dress. Thank God, the minute I found out about this interview last week, I had the presence of mind—right after puking into a trashcan, of course—to make an appointment with a celebrity stylist to get myself downright Penelope-cized. I still look like me, which is good—and unavoidable. But it's the best and sexiest version of me ever. It's amazing what a difference flattering clothes, come-fuck-me heels, a sassy haircut, and blond highlights can make! I look down at my dress and the butterflies in my stomach momentarily stop flapping to give each other high fives. High *wings*?

"Are you dying to hear some new music from Lucas Ford?" the DJ's voice on the radio asks as the Justin Timberlake song ends.

My head snaps up from my notes and the hair on the back of my neck stands up.

"I've got the first single off Luke's upcoming album, which will be releasing in three months," the DJ continues. "And folks, if this first single is any indication of what we can expect from the full album, this is going to be Lucas Ford's best album yet. So, here it is... Lucas Ford and his brand new, heart-wrenching song, 'Abandoned.'"

The cab driver turns up the volume. "I love Lucas Ford."

I don't reply. I'm too excited to speak. Or breathe.

The song kicks off with a guitar riff that's so quintessential Lucas Ford, I'd know it was him playing it even if the DJ hadn't said so.

My heart is racing from the guitar riff alone, but when Lucas begins to sing, it explodes and splatters all over the inside of the cab. *Wow.*

Lucas's voice is raw and vulnerable and sexy in a whole new way in this song. Yes, there's something reminiscent of "Shattered Hearts" in the way he's singing, but he's a grown man of almost thirty now, after all, and the power and depth of his voice is something entirely new.

"Abandoned," Lucas sings. "I wasn't the man for you. Abandoned. You followed the plan straight through. Abandoned. And now there's nothing I can do. Oh, baby, I've been abandoned by you."

Tears prick my eyes as I continue to listen to the heartbreaking song. It's passionate. Excruciating. Tormented. *Utterly beautiful.* And I never want to hear the motherfucking thing again.

"Wow," the cabbie says breezily when the song ends. "That was even better than 'Shattered Hearts,' don't you think? It kinda reminds me of that one. Same kinda thing, you know? But even better. I like the melody. It's catchy."

I nod and try to smile at the driver's eyes looking at me in his rearview mirror, but I'm too overcome to command my vocal cords.

"Good for him," the driver says, apparently not fazed by my silence. "I was hoping for a comeback for him. I love Lucas."

I wipe my eyes and find my voice. "Yeah. So do I."

CHAPTER THIRTY-FIVE

I settle into the back seat of the black sedan that's driving me to work from my overnight stay at the Ritz Carlton and immediately pull my phone and earbuds out of my bag. It's been a year since Lucas excitedly told the audience at his LA concert he'd written a bunch of songs for his fourth album, and three months since I heard "Abandoned" in the back of that taxi. Finally, Lucas's fourth album is here.

The album released at midnight last night, actually, and although I'd planned to stay awake and download the whole thing at twelve oh one, it wasn't meant to be. Unfortunately—or fortunately—my plan to listen to Lucas's album on repeat last night was shot to hell. Around eleven, Brandon, my so-called boyfriend—or glorified fuck buddy—of the past three months, ever since that fateful day I interviewed him, called to say he'd spontaneously managed to squeeze a couple nights' stay in New York into his filming schedule. He said he'd been "jonesing to tie up his kinky little cutie and fuck her to within an inch of her life." Of course, since I can't resist a confident man who orders me into his bed, I immediately changed out of my flannel jammies and fuzzy socks and into something appropriately Penelope-ish, and traipsed off from my Brooklyn apartment to the Ritz Carlton in Manhattan for our unexpected rendezvous. And then, yes, I did all manner of kinky things with Mr. Movie Star all night long. Just the way he likes it, the dirty bastard.

As Lucas's album continues downloading onto my phone, I text my therapist to confirm my appointment after work. Who knew there were wonderful people in the profession who listen kindly and without judgment to their patients' thoughts and concerns? As amazing as it sounds, I've been going to Dr. Amy for six months now and she hasn't called me "abnormal" or "aberrant" even once! In fact, I can't even count the number of times Dr. Amy's waved her hand dismissively at me and said, "Oh, Abby, honey, that's perfectly normal!"

I peek impatiently at Lucas's album as it continues to download and my stomach flips over with anticipation. The album is called *From A...to Me*, and it features songs that are all one-word titles starting with the letter *A*.

Of course, the first *A* song on the album is the already-released single, "Abandoned," which I've now heard at least ten thousand times in three months, despite my best efforts to avoid it like the plague.

Oh, lord, how I've tried not to hear "Abandoned" since that first time in the taxi on my way to interview Brandon three months ago. But not hearing that beautiful, heart-wrenching song everywhere was literally impossible. Why? Because I live on planet Earth and "Abandoned" is a smash hit, the kind of song you can't help hearing *everywhere* you go, every hour on the hour—on the radio, in TV commercials, in cabs and banks and restaurants and grocery stores and from passing cars. At this point, the song is simply part of the air we humans breathe. An accepted part of the atmosphere.

But, of course, "Abandoned" isn't the only *A* song on Lucas's new album. There are twelve more. "Ass-kicker," "Assassin," "Ambushed," "Angel," "Ashamed," "Aberration," "Addicted," "Aroma," "Alive," "Ache," "Adore," and..."Abby."

Oh, God, these song titles!

Even without hearing the actual songs, I know they're going to decimate me.

Finally, the full album is downloaded.

I close my eyes and gather myself for a moment before pressing play. I don't know why, but after a full year and four published articles for *Maxim*—including my rather feisty interview of Brandon—I thought I'd have heard from Lucas by now. If I'm being perfectly honest, I kind of thought Lucas would have sent me an early copy of the album with a little note, or would have shown up at *Maxim*'s headquarters with a signed copy, saying, "Hey, Abby! One day is finally here, baby!" But nope. Not a word from Mr. Rock Star in a full year. Apparently, Lucas intends to do all his talking to me through his songs.

I lean back into the cushy leather seat of the sedan, push my earbuds firmly into my ears, and press play on my first song selection. It's not the first track listed on the album, of course. It's actually the last. But it's the first song I want to hear. "Abby."

CHAPTER THIRTY-SIX

I settle onto my couch in front of my TV in my flannel pajamas and fuzzy socks, a glass of wine and Lucas's handwritten note to me from a year and a half ago in my hands. It's Grammy time and the red carpet entrances at Madison Square Garden are just getting underway.

Holy fuckballs, my stomach's in knots. Please, God, let Lucas win a truckload of Grammys tonight like everyone keeps predicting he will.

Oh, there's Justin Timberlake! So handsome and talented and funny. Gah. Love him.

And there's Adele! Oh my gosh, I adore her. She's perfect.

I clutch my handwritten note from Lucas as a good luck charm and chomp some popcorn from a bowl on the coffee table, watching artist after artist getting interviewed by a virtual army of journalists on the red carpet. Damn. I'm suddenly second-guessing my decision to turn down working the red carpet tonight. Why did I do that again? Oh, yeah, because the thought of seeing Lucas again for the first time in a year and a half—for no more than thirty seconds amid flashing bulbs and people screaming to get his attention—made me feel physically ill. If ever I'm going to see that beautiful man again—*please, God, yes*—I want to be able to converse with him in a meaningful way. I owe my new amazing life to him, after all. Everything that I am, everything I've become, every time I lay my head on my pillow, smiling from ear to ear, I owe it all to him. If ever I get to see Lucas again, I want to be able to pour my heart out to him and thank him from the bottom of my soul, and not ask him a rote question while standing in line with fifty other journalists on a red carpet.

I take a long sip of my wine, my stomach tight with anticipation. Oh, what I wouldn't give to see Lucas again in a meaningful way. Even if only for fifteen minutes. Just to hug him and tell him his unbelievable gift saved my life.

The red carpet portion of the evening is almost over now. Where the heck is he? Is he making a grand entrance at the last possible moment...or skipping the red carpet altogether?

On a sudden impulse, I open Lucas's notecard to me and touch his angular script, overcome with the need to connect with him tonight of all nights in any way I can, even if only by touching something that proves I didn't imagine our magical time together.

I hope our paths cross again one day in NYC, I truly do, he wrote to me. *But only if you're a writer, making your dreams come true. I wish you the best, always and forever.*   *Luke.*

Why the heck did he write those words if he was never going to contact me again? I mean, shit, if one day hasn't arrived by now, I'm pretty sure it never will. Thanks to Lucas and his staggering generosity, I've now lived in New York for almost a year and a half, a full year of that as a professional writer. My blog is more popular than ever and I've published a whole bunch of articles. Not just in *Maxim,* but in some of its sister publications, too. Wouldn't Lucas know about all of that? I mean, I have no delusions he's been stalking me online, but at the very least, I'd have thought he'd have checked in on me once or twice to see what I was up to, if only to follow up on his two hundred fifty thousand bucks.

And when I let myself get really carried away with my fantasies, I must admit I imagine Lucas showing up at *Maxim*'s offices in Manhattan to declare his love for me. Oh, I don't know. I don't have any means of contacting him, after all. I'm sure it'd be easier to get the Pope's personal cell phone number than Lucas Ford's. Clearly, if one day is ever going to arrive, it's up to him to make it happen. He did write in his note he truly hopes our paths cross again, after all. *So why hasn't he tracked me down?*

I've no sooner asked myself that question than Lucas appears on the red carpet to implicitly answer it for me.

Well, gosh, Abby, it seems I've been too busy making Grammy-nominated music and fucking the German supermodel who's currently hanging on my arm to spend even a half second thinking about some hotel clerk from Miami... oh, sorry, Denver... whom I briefly role-played with a lifetime ago. But, hey, I wish you the best, always and forever! Luke.

CHAPTER THIRTY-SEVEN

I board my new train—the Q train from Brooklyn to Manhattan—and settle in for my hour-and-a-half commute. It's a fairly long commute every day, true, but it's a small price to pay to get to live in the greatest city in the world and work at my dream job. And, on my writer's salary, living in Manhattan is simply out of the question. Plus, my long commute every day gives me time to write on my laptop or read a book or listen to music, all of which I love to do.

This morning, especially, I don't mind the train ride. Despite the rough start to the Grammys telecast last night—*fuck you, German supermodel*—I couldn't help but feel nothing but euphoria once the show got underway and Lucas started racking up win after win. Among his other awards, Lucas took top honors for song of the year, record of the year, and album of the year. And, God, he looked so *happy* accepting all of them!

So, in celebration of Lucas's well-deserved night of triumph, I've decided to sit back during this entire train ride and listen to *From A...to Me* all the way through, again and again, and savor every single glorious sound. Hell, I'm even going to listen to "Abandoned," though I've previously sworn never to purposefully hear that excruciating song ever again.

I feel high today, honestly. So happy for Lucas, I can barely function. For some reason, watching him win all those awards gave me more than a thrill. It gave me peace. Above anything else I might feel about Lucas, I truly want him to be happy. Period.

And, as I saw last night, he is.

But, of course, I also want myself to be happy, too. And that's why I've decided to let go of my dream of ever seeing Lucas again. I realized last night, maintaining hope is holding me back from finding true love with someone else. And, crazy as it sounds, I suddenly feel like my heart is genuinely ready to find true love. Healthy, true love. Not fun with a fuck buddy. Not a fling or illicit tryst. Not some bad boy who's going to throw me away. Not a movie star who swoops into town out of nowhere or sends a private plane for me to meet him in Jamaica. I want love with a genuinely kind person who adores me for who I am and treats me well, no tropical destinations required. And, by God, that's what I'm going to find for myself. And, sadly, that means I need to move on from fantasizing about one day with Lucas Ford.

Do I wish things might have worked out differently for Lucas and me, like in a fairytale? Yes, I do. Of course. But after what he said to me in his first of many acceptance speeches last night, I finally felt like I had the closure I've needed for so long in order to move on. Bottom line—when Lucas spoke to me through my TV last night, he set me free. And I'm grateful for it.

I nestle into my seat on the train and press play on the first song on Lucas's album, letting his guitar playing and beautiful, soulful voice flood me. And as Lucas serenades me, I close my eyes and think about Lucas's first acceptance speech last night. The one during which he looked right into the camera, like he was talking directly to me, and said, "I'd especially like to thank the woman who inspired every song on this album. Abby, I couldn't have written these songs without you and our time together in Penthouse A. Without the piece of your heart you so generously gave me. And for that, I'll always love you, Abby. Thank you so much for being my muse. And for so much more than that. For telling me the truth when I needed to hear it most. Thank you for everything."

Yeah, I pretty much died.

And, I admit it, a large piece of me felt wickedly happy to think his supermodel girlfriend was sitting in the front row, listening to him say those unbelievable words to some mystery chick named Abby who did God knows what with him in Penthouse A. But, of course, on the downside, I also knew by the way Lucas had phrased his remarks, he was telling me he loved me as his muse and nothing more. The artist inside him loves me and always will. But the man? Not so much.

And, for some reason, in that moment, that was enough for me. Slightly sad, yes. Not ideal, true... But enough. Hey, I've got to figure there are worse things in the world than being the woman Lucas Ford will "always love" for inspiring one of the greatest and most decorated albums in the history of music.

Of course, I was glued to the entire broadcast for the rest of the night, hoping Lucas might mention me again. Or *maybe* declare his undying love to me in words even bolder than those he'd used in his first speech. But Lucas never spoke to me again. Instead, he used every other speech of the night to effusively thank his "awesome" fans and tell them how "grateful" he is for their "never-ending love and support."

And, strangely, by the end of the show, I felt so at peace. Ready to move on and find a man willing to commit to me today—and not just some possible-but-not-guaranteed one day. I called my on-again-off-again movie star boyfriend and told him it had been a super fun ride and he'd been truly lovely to me and always ridiculously generous, but that I was ready to move on to something healthy. To start looking for a serious commitment from someone roughly my own age. He handled the break up remarkably well.

And, now, as I sit on my train, headed into work, I feel light as a feather. Inexplicably free of every demon that's ever haunted me my whole life—not to mention hopeful and excited about my future. I can't wait to see whatever or whoever awaits me in this big, beautiful world. And I truly believe I have Lucas Ford to thank for that.

About five minutes from my stop, I indulge myself and press play on "Abby" for a third time this train ride. This will be the last time I listen to this song, I decide. Because listening to it over and over again and dreaming about what might have been one day for Lucas and me simply isn't healthy for my soul. And so, with a wistful sigh, I push my earbuds firmly into my ears, close my eyes, and lose myself in Lucas singing "Abby" to me for the very last time.

Maybe we weren't meant to be
In this lifetime or the next two or three
But I still believe we're meant to be
In the fourth or fifth or in a dream
Maybe up in heaven where the angels sing?
Maybe
Abby

One day
I'll wrap my arms around your wings
And stroke your feathers and tell you things
About how much you mean to me
And how you showed me A to me
Maybe
Abby
One day
Oh, Abby, I'm just a broken slave
Chained to the muse with debts to pay
A mountain of IOUs, my cage
So many dragons left to slay
But maybe
Abby
One day
I'll live and learn my way to you
And won't be scared to tell the truth
I'll hunt you down, unveil my plan
And stroke your wings and be your man
Maybe
Abby
One day
But truth be told I'm afraid, my dear
You'll say I wasn't worth the pain
Not worthy of the heart I gave
An endless pit that takes and takes
Maybe
Abby

One day
I'm afraid that's what you'll say to me
And, worse, you'll say it honestly
Same way you say everything
Jolt me with reality
Maybe
Abby
One day
I hate to say it 'cause it's cliché
Hate to say what causes pain
'It's not you, it's me, my dear,'
Me, me, me, me, me
Couldn't love the way you did, Abby
'Cause I was your teenage fantasy
But none of it was real, you see
Nothing but a dream
But maybe
Abby
One day
When my soul is finally free
Not a barter or commodity
When I don't bleed so damned easily
Then brave is what I'll be
Maybe
Abby
One day
And if not
My dearest Abby

Maybe
One day
One day
One day
Maybe you'll forgive me.

The song ends just as my train pulls to my stop.

I wipe my eyes and cheeks. "I forgive you, Lucas," I whisper, my words swallowed by the commotion in the train and the hustle and bustle of commuters around me. "Be happy."

I stand, put my phone in my pocket, bundle up in my scarf, gloves, and thick wool coat, wipe my eyes and cheeks again, and start walking the four blocks to my office building.

As I enter the lobby of my building, my phone buzzes in my pocket. I pull off my gloves and grab my phone. It's a text from my boss that makes my heart stop.

Come to my office the minute you get in! You hit the motherlode, Abby! LUCAS FORD!!!!!!!!!!!!!

CHAPTER THIRTY-EIGHT

"He called *me,* Abby, not the other way around!" my boss shouts as I enter his office. "And it was Lucas Ford calling me *personally*, not his publicist!"

I clutch my heart, feeling like I'm about to pass out. "What'd he say?"

"He offered an *exclusive* interview about his Grammy wins and anything else we want to ask him about. He said *no* topic is off limits. *Nothing.* His only condition? None other than Penelope Pleasure has to conduct the interview and it has to be done today at his hotel because he's heading back to LA tomorrow morning. He said he read your interview of Brandon Hanover and he wants 'the exact same treatment'!"

My brain is short-circuiting. Lucas wants to see me? *Today*? And he read my interview of Mr. Movie Star and "wants the exact same treatment"? Gah! My mind is racing. Does that mean Lucas knows about my so-called relationship with Brandon? And if so, was his choice of words his way of telling me our one day has finally arrived? Or did he call my boss simply because he wants to help my career again, and nothing more?

"Do you know him?" my boss asks as we settle into seats on opposite sides of his large desk.

I shake my head like a little kid accused of stealing a cookie.

My boss smirks. "No? Huh. I thought maybe, just maybe, you were the 'Abby' from the song."

I try to chuckle breezily but, surely, I sound more like a llama with bronchitis. "Nope. I wish."

"Hey, it's not *ridiculous* to think the song might be about you. You snagged Brandon Hanover, so why not Lucas Ford, too?" He winks.

"Aw, don't believe those pesky rumors about Brandon Hanover and me," I say coyly, but we both know I'm full of it. It's become a bit of a running gag between us that I won't cop to any manner of personal relationship with Mr. Movie Star. Not because Brandon would care, by the way. But because, one, I don't want to be known as yet another one of Brandon Hanover's many playthings, and, two, I'd always figured the less people knew about my so-called relationship with him, the less chance paparazzi would've kept me in the frame if he happened to be leaving a restaurant with me.

My boss looks at me sideways. "Are you sure you've never met Lucas Ford?"

"I'm sure," I say. "I've always wanted to meet him, though. He's my idea of the perfect man."

"Mine, too," my boss says.

"I had a massive crush on him as a teenager," I say.

"Me, too. But as an adult."

We both laugh.

"Did you watch the Grammys last night?" my boss asks.

"Of course. He deserved every award he won."

"Yeah, I noticed he thanked a girl named Abby and mentioned

time they spent together in Penthouse A."

My face suddenly feels hot. "Oh, yeah. I saw that, too."

My boss beams an adorable smile at me. "Wasn't it Denver where you worked at a hotel before coming to New York?"

I nod, feeling like my throat is closing up.

"I thought so," my boss says, a gleam in his eyes. "Did the hotel where you worked have a Penthouse A?"

I narrow my eyes and don't respond.

My boss grins. "I did a little Googling last night and it turns out it was Denver where Lucas Ford had that meltdown of his. And then, a few weeks after that, he was bright-eyed and bushy-tailed at a concert in LA, telling everyone he'd just written a bunch of new songs over the prior few weeks. And then last night, I'll be damned, he thanked a woman named Abby and referenced some magical time in Penthouse A as the inspiration for all the songs on the album." He playfully mimics the glare I'm throwing at him. "And now, imagine that, he's calling to say he wants Penelope Pleasure *and no one else* to interview him."

I try not to let my face give anything away. "Imagine that."

My boss continues. "And you want to know the weirdest thing that happened when I spoke to him? Something I forgot to mention?" He smiles deviously.

"Sure."

"A couple times during my very short conversation with Lucas Ford, he referred to you as *Abby,* and *not* Penelope."

I feel my eyes bugging out of my head but remain mute.

"And that kind of confuses me, to be honest," my boss adds. "How on earth would Lucas Ford know your real name is Abby, Miss

Pleasure? I've never seen you advertise that."

I'm working very hard not to return my boss's smug smile. "I have no idea," I say. "But he's Lucas Ford, after all. He's obviously got people who know things." I stand abruptly. "Anything else I need to know before I head over to his hotel? The Four Seasons, did you say?"

My boss's smile broadens. "Yeah, he's checked in under the name Jacob Knobhopper, and he's staying in none other than Penthouse A."

I don't know what facial expression is involuntarily overtaking my features right now, but whatever it is, it's causing my boss to let out a loud whoop of pure glee. "Oh, Abby," he says affectionately. "Have I ever told you I love you more than life itself?"

I can't help myself. I return his beaming smile. "Yes, you have, thank God. Many, many times."

My boss comes around his desk and hugs me. "You never cease to amaze me, Penelope." He looks at his watch. "Okay, you'd better get going, honey. You'll get there on the early side if you leave now, but that's good. I've heard Lucas Ford's a bit of an impatient prick and we don't want to keep him waiting." At that, he flashes me another mischievous smile. Clearly, he's trying to bait me into defending Lucas's honor, the same way he's tried to bait me for the past year to defend Brandon's. But I'm not going to fall for it and he knows it.

I look down at my dress, relieved I happened to have picked out a particularly "Penelope-esque" dress today, and run my fingertips through my blond pixie cut. "Do I look okay? Am I Lucas-Ford-worthy, you think?"

"You're perfect from head to toe, sweetheart. Seriously, honey, if Lucas Ford doesn't fall head over heels in love with you the minute he sees you, then he's secretly batting for my team."

CHAPTER THIRTY-NINE

"Penthouse A is the last door at the end of the hallway," says the hotel employee who is escorting me to the restricted penthouse floor. He gestures through the opened elevator doors. "Do you require an escort all the way to Mr. Knobhopper's door, miss?"

We smile at each other about Lucas's ridiculous pseudonym. "No, I'm good," I say. "Mr. Knobhopper is expecting me. Thank you."

I begin walking down the short hallway, my knees wobbling and my mind racing. Does Lucas truly expect me to *interview* him today or could it be, please God, that today is finally one day?

I reach the door of the penthouse.

Oh, lord, my heart is pounding.

I stand and stare at the door for a ridiculously long amount of time, feeling sick to my stomach. If I'm seriously here to interview Lucas and nothing more, if he hasn't summoned me here because he's been aching for our one day as much as I have over the past year and a half, I'll be heartbroken.

I take another deep breath.

Well, crap, no matter how scared I am, I can't stand out here forever.

I rap softly on the penthouse door. Ten seconds later, lo and behold, Nerd Guy, who checked Lucas into The Rockford a lifetime ago, is standing before me.

I put out my hand. "Hi there. I'm Penelope Pleasure. Abby Medford, actually. I'm here to interview Mr. Ford, at his request."

It's clear from Nerd Guy's expression he doesn't recognize me in the slightest. "Yeah. Come in." He widens the door to reveal a penthouse suite that blows the one from The Rockford out of the water. "Luke will be out in a minute. He's on the phone in the bedroom." Nerd Guy motions to a sitting area. "Can I get you something to drink while you wait? Water? Beer? Booze? Wine?"

"Water would be great," I say. "Thank you."

I settle myself onto the couch, trying desperately to breathe.

There's a woman talking on the phone at a little desk in the corner, and from the professional but firm tone of her voice, it sounds to me like she's very calmly kicking someone's ass. There are a couple of extremely large dudes sitting in a far corner. Bodyguards? And there's another nerdy dude sitting in an armchair a few feet away from mine. But no German supermodel, as far as I can see. Huh. Maybe "Lucas is talking on the phone in the bedroom" is code for "Lucas is busy fucking a German supermodel up the ass in the bedroom."

I smile politely at Nerd Guy Number Two sitting a few feet away from me in the sitting area. "Hi there," I say. "I'm Abby."

His face lights up with some sort of recognition. "Jeremy." He leans forward and shakes my hand. "Luke's manager. He told me about you. Nice to finally meet you."

The hair on my arms stands up. *What did Lucas say about me?*

Nerd Guy Number Two motions to the woman on the phone in the corner. "That's Luke's publicist. I'm sure she'll want to talk to you about the ground rules for the interview when she gets off the phone."

My chest squeezes. Crap. Does that mean I'm really here to do an interview?

The original Nerd Guy returns and hands me a glass of ice water.

"Thank you," I say. I look at Nerd Guy Number Two. "I only just found out about the interview an hour ago, so...um...I was just planning to talk to Lucas organically. But, of course, I'd be happy to ask, or refrain from asking, whatever you guys want. I didn't make a pitch to get the interview. Lucas called my boss and..." I trail off and stand abruptly. Lucas has just come out of the bedroom, and every single cell in my body is physically straining toward his beautiful frame.

Oh, dear lord, he's stunning. Ten times more gorgeous than he ever was when he pretended to be my boyfriend. He looks like a new man. He looks...*happy.*

Lucas strides toward me, his eyes blazing, his cheeks flushed. But before he reaches me, his publicist, who just happened to get off her call as Lucas appeared, is standing in front of me, her hand out.

The publicist introduces herself to me, seemingly oblivious to the fact that she just cock-blocked her famous client.

I take the publicist's hand and shake it, but I'm focused on Lucas's handsome face.

"So, let's talk ground rules for the interview," the publicist barks. "Have a seat." She motions to the couch.

"Let's not," Lucas says behind her, looking like he's about to explode. "In fact, you can all clear out. I think this particular interview should be done one-on-one."

Lucas's entourage looks at each other, obviously taken aback.

"Bye, everyone," Lucas says, still looking right at me. "Thanks."

The publicist looks me up and down, clearly surprised, and then looks at her client. "You sure, Lucas? I'd like to—"

"I'm sure."

Slowly, everyone around us gathers their stuff and shuffles out the door, all of them glancing at each other as though they're deeply offended by Lucas's request.

The door clicks softly.

And everyone is gone.

I look at Lucas, unsure what to do. Of course, the only thing my body wants to do is hurl myself into his arms. But I refrain. For all I know, Lucas's supermodel girlfriend is in the bedroom and I'm here to do a freaking interview.

"Sit," Lucas says.

I sit on one end of the couch and Lucas sits on the other.

"You look gorgeous," he says, his eyes burning.

"Thank you. So do you. Better than ever. I'm so proud of you."

Lucas looks me up and down again, his eyes on fire. "You were always pretty, don't get me wrong, but wow, Abby, with that hair and those clothes, you actually look like an assassin now. I love it."

I bite my lower lip and run my fingers through my hair. "Thank you." I wink. "I'm Penelope Pleasure now, you know. And she's sassy."

Lucas laughs. "Yes, she is."

I shift in my seat. My God, my heartbeat is absolutely pounding in my ears. For the life of me, I can't read Lucas's body language. Is he keeping his distance over there on the other end of the couch because his girlfriend is in the bedroom? Or because this truly is a professional opportunity he's extending to me? I truly have no idea what's going on. But suddenly I can't contain the tidal wave of emotion rising up inside me. "Thank you so much for the money," I blurt. "I didn't have your phone number to thank you, so I sent a card to the return address on the FedEx envelope. I had no other way to contact you. You've changed my life. I've been dying to thank you."

Lucas smiles. "I got your card. It was sweet. You're very welcome."

Tears prick my eyes. "I'll never be able to thank you enough for what you've done for me. Lucas, you saved me."

"All I did was return the favor after you saved me."

"But Lucas, you had no favor to return. You're the one who wrote those amazing songs, not me. I did nothing. I don't deserve thanks. But you? Your generosity and belief in me changed the trajectory of my entire life." I swallow hard. "You saved me from what was sure to be a life of misery and extreme lack of fulfillment. You saved me, Lucas. And now I'm genuinely happy."

Lucas's face melts. "I'm so glad to hear it. But Angel, trust me. You saved yourself. I just gave you a tiny nudge. You did it yourself."

"A tiny nudge? No, Lucas, you pushed me off a cliff. You gave me an insane amount of money. I guarantee you, I wouldn't have taken a leap of faith without that money. And even more so, without you telling me I was talented."

"I just spoke the truth. You've got a gift."

"But you backed up your belief in me with so much money."

"It was nothing. I've got more money than God these days. I don't know if you've heard, but since we last saw each other, I've had a couple hit songs."

I chuckle and wipe my eyes. "Really? No, I don't think I've heard about that. Congrats."

He smiles. "So how'd your parents take it when you quit law school?"

I glance toward the bedroom, trying to figure out if a certain German supermodel is holed up in there, but I can't see inside the cracked door from here. "My parents freaked the fuck out, actually," I say and he laughs. "They thought me quitting school was a sign I was flying off the rails and 'making unhealthy choices' again." I roll my eyes at the memory. "They wanted to check me into some sort of rehab facility when I first told them my plans. But now that I'm gainfully employed and there are no signs I'm a human grenade, they're vaguely tolerant of my life choices. Maybe even a tiny bit proud. Sort of."

"You still talk to them?"

I nod. "It's strained, to be honest. But at least they've recently stopped trying to convince me to go back to law school."

"And your demons? How are they holding up?"

Why aren't we in each other's arms, kissing the hell out of each other? Why is this conversation so...polite? "They're my little bitches," I say. "I've been in therapy with this amazing woman in the city for a while now, and I've never been better. Honestly, I do what I want and I don't feel like I have any issues anymore. It turns out, being happy and honest about who I am in all aspects of my life has worked some sort of exorcism on those pesky little demons. Who knew honesty and happiness were the magic bullets?"

Lucas smiles broadly. "Fantastic." He pauses. "So...speaking of pesky demons, did you get a chance to listen to my song 'Abby'?"

Boom. Here we go. Finally. "Only a couple...*billion* times," I say. "I listened to it four times this morning, actually."

Lucas looks nervous. "And?"

And what do you think, motherfucker? I'm wondering if today is finally one day!

"And...it ripped my heart out while simultaneously giving me hope," I answer honestly. "It made me wonder if maybe, one day, we might get to connect again."

"And now here we are," he says.

I open my mouth and close it. What the heck does that mean? Is this our one day or not? If I don't find out what's going on soon, I'm seriously going to lose my mind.

"So, hey, whatever happened to you hating paparazzi?" Lucas asks. His jaw muscles pulse. "I keep seeing photos of you coming out of restaurants and bars with Brandon Hard-on. What's that about?"

And suddenly this strangeness between us makes perfect sense. Lucas thinks I'm in love with Brandon Hanover! "I'm really glad you brought that up," I say. "I actually have a confession to make about that."

Lucas looks like he's holding his breath.

"Remember that time I told you I hated paparazzi? That was a bald-faced lie. I'm a famewhore of the highest order, Lucas. Fame, fame, fame! That's all I care about. I crave it like a junkie craves smack."

Lucas laughs. "I knew it!" He bites his beautiful lip and looks at me ruefully. "So I presume you've been rocking that fucker's world, the same way you rocked mine?"

My heart leaps. *I rocked Lucas's world?* "Yeah, I rocked

Brandon's world," I admit. "But not emotionally. Only physically. Our relationship, such as it was, was about as deep as a puddle."

Lucas's face lights up. "*Was*? You're not with him anymore?"

I grin broadly. "I officially ended things with him last night. Right after watching the Grammys, as a matter of fact."

He looks absolutely electrified. "Really? Why'd you do that?"

"When you thanked me in your first speech, something clicked inside me. I realized I deserve more than being someone's glorified fuck buddy. I realized I want something real."

The look Lucas is flashing me could melt the polar ice caps. "What'd Brandon Hand Job say when you told him you were done with him?"

"He said, 'Okay.'"

Lucas laughs. "Wow. Deep thoughts from Mr. Action Hero."

"Well, in his defense, he also generously offered to buy me an apartment in the city as a parting gift."

An unmistakable shadow crosses over Lucas's face. "And what'd you say to that offer?"

"I said, 'No, thank you.' I didn't want him assuming he had any sort of claim over me going forward. I wanted to be completely free."

We stare at each other for some time, the sexual tension between us thick.

"Speaking of fuck buddies," I say, "whatever happened to you never dating supermodels?"

He smiles wickedly. "Oh, you saw me with Bridgette last night, did you?"

"She was your date at the *Grammys,* Lucas. Literally half the world's population saw you with her."

He smirks. "Were you jealous?"

"I'll put it this way. I would have been quite pleased if there had been a vat of acid on the red carpet last night and she had tripped and stumbled into it."

Lucas throws his head back and laughs. "Yeah, me too. She's such a bitch, you have no idea. God, I hate that woman."

I might explode with happiness. I want to throw myself at him, but I just can't be sure I won't be rejected.

Lucas sighs. "Come here, Ass-kicker." He pats the couch next to him and I warily scoot closer. He grabs my hand and electricity shoots throughout my body, straight into my crotch. "Angel," he says. "Remember what I told you? I show up places with models and actresses sometimes for *publicity*. Bridgette and I made for good TV last night, didn't we? I'm told by my publicist we're 'the perfect couple.'"

The weight of the world just lifted off me. "So you're single?"

"I'm single. Just like you. Free as a bird." But still he doesn't make his move the way I'm hoping he will. He simply begins stroking my forearm gently. "Why didn't you write that hit piece about me, Abby?" he asks softly. "I kept checking your blog, and then *Maxim*, looking for it. I kept waiting for my lawyer to call and tell me there was something really embarrassing I needed to see...but it never came."

I shrug.

"Why didn't you write it, Abby?"

"Because I'd never do that to you," I say simply. "Never."

He touches my cheek tenderly. "Why not? Everybody uses me. And I gave you permission. So why not you, too?"

I look into his glistening eyes. He truly doesn't understand why I didn't want to use our magical time together for personal gain? Well, then I guess I'll just have to explain it to him in unambiguous terms. "I didn't write it because I love you, Lucas," I say. "I genuinely love you. I'd never use you or the way I feel about you to *get* something for myself. The only thing I want from you is for you to be happy, whether that includes me or not."

And that's it. A dam visibly breaks inside him. He grabs my face and kisses me so passionately he takes my breath away.

I throw my arms around him, straddle his lap, and return his kiss, surrendering myself to him, letting my lips and tongue and body tell him everything my paltry words can't. I love him and I always will. I love the fantasy of him. The reality of him. The artist. The man. I love him whether today is one day or just a sweet chance for closure. No matter the circumstance, I'll love this man until the day I die.

In a frenzy of heat and want and near-desperate need, Lucas breaks free of my hungry kiss and begins frantically pulling the hem of my dress up while I begin feverishly unbuttoning his jeans in response.

Lucas's hard cock pops out of his jeans, its tip shiny and beautiful. He sits up slightly, tossing me off him so he can pull off his jeans and shirt, and I finish getting my dress off.

I peel my bra and undies off in a flash.

He yanks off his briefs with a grunt.

Finally, we're both naked, our skin covered in goosebumps, our eyes blazing.

He scoops me up and carries my naked body in his arms toward the bedroom.

"I haven't stopped thinking about you in all this time," he breathes. "I've been with so many women since you, trying to forget you, trying to convince myself what happened between us wasn't real, but nobody's made me feel the way you did." He lays me onto the mattress. "You're the only one who makes me feel completely alive, Abby. The only one." His mouth is on mine. His naked body is hulking over mine. His forearms are on either side of my head on the mattress as he presses himself against me and juts his hard-on into my entrance. "You still on the pill, Angel?"

I nod and grip his face, my body already on the cusp of release. In seconds, I feel the delectable sensation of his body burrowing inside mine, and then the feeling of his hard shaft thrusting deep, deep, deep inside me. His lips are on mine. His tongue is in my mouth. His hard chest is smashing into my breasts. And all of it is sending me into ecstasy.

"It was real," Lucas whispers into my ear, almost inaudibly. "Now I know. It was real, Abby. And one in a million."

I throw my arms around him, grind my hips into his, and lose myself to waves of pleasure rippling throughout my core.

He makes love to me at first, whispering words of adoration into my ear. But soon we're fucking like wild animals, both of us growling and groaning and screaming each other's names. When he finally comes, he comes hard and inside me, a mangled cry of release and relief escaping his beautiful lips.

When we're both spent, we lie in the bed together for a long time, stroking each other, kissing and laughing.

"So is this one day?" I whisper.

"Fuck yeah," Lucas says, nuzzling his nose into mine. "I've lived and learned my way to you and now I'm stroking your wings and being your man."

My heart leaps. "You're my man?"

"All yours."

My heart is physically palpitating. "I should warn you," I say. "I don't want a fling, not even with you. I want something committed and exclusive or nothing at all. Anything less will be torture for me."

Lucas grins broadly and strokes my arm. "As far as I'm concerned, I'm not letting you out of my sight from here on out."

I flash him a shy smile. "You're not?"

"Hell no. You're mine. You're coming to LA with me tomorrow. And from there, in a couple weeks, you're joining me on my world tour."

"You're going on a world tour?"

"For a year. And you're coming with me."

I'm suddenly anxious. "But I've got a job, Lucas. A job I love."

Lucas shrugs. "So do your job on the road. You're a writer. Write about the tour or me or whatever you see on our adventures, just as long as you don't leave my side." He nuzzles his nose into my hair and inhales deeply. "I fucked up when I let you go and I'm not gonna do that again."

"But what about my apartment? I signed a year's lease."

"Have you heard a word I've said? You don't need an apartment because you're going to live with me. Where I go, you go. I'll pay off your lease."

I kiss his beautiful lips. "But what about when the tour is over? Maybe I should keep my apartment for when we get back, just in case I need it?"

"Abby, listen to me. Get it through your head. After the tour, you're going to live with *me*. You're mine. I'm yours. It's you and me from now on and no one else."

I bite my lip, overwhelmed.

Lucas suddenly looks anxious. "You're on board for all that, right?" He pauses. "Abby, seriously, you've got to say yes or I'm gonna be crushed."

I touch his cheek. "Yes."

Lucas exhales loudly. "Jesus. You scared me for a second there."

"Oh, please. You had to have known I'd say yes."

"I had no idea what you'd say. You're Penelope Pleasure, dating that asshole. And I knew 'Abby' had to be a bit of a mind-fuck for you." He shrugs. "I honestly thought it was fifty-fifty you'd tell me to fuck off."

I stroke his face. "I'm all yours, baby. I was yours the minute you walked into The Rockford. I'm yours now."

"Oh, Jesus," Lucas says, sitting up abruptly in the bed. "The muse is back!" He leaps out of bed and lurches toward the living area but abruptly stops short and lopes back to me, laughing. "You're not allowed to leave my side, remember?" He scoops my naked body off the mattress and carries me into the living area, where he places me gently on the couch with a kiss. "Now don't move a muscle. You'll be my Kate Winslet and I'm your Leonardo DiCaprio while I write this kick-ass song."

I laugh and adopt Kate Winslet's reclining pose from *Titanic* as Lucas settles himself on the other end of the couch with his guitar.

He plays a catchy little riff. "Oh, man, this is going to be a good one," he says. He plays the riff again.

"What's it called?" I ask.

"'I'm Yours.'"

I cringe.

"No?"

"I'm pretty sure Jason Mraz has cornered the market on that song title."

"Fuck. I forgot about that motherfucker. *Damn.*" He plays his riff again, looking thoughtful. "Well, shit. That would have been the perfect title for this one, seeing as how I'm yours and all."

"Well, thank you for the sentiment. I appreciate it. But Jason beat you to it."

Lucas smiles as he strums. "Okay, no big deal. I'm really good at this songwriting thing, remember? I've won Grammys and everything." He strums for a moment. "Okay, I've got a badass new title for it, just that fast. 'Tiny Dancer.'"

I laugh and shake my head.

"No?" Lucas asks with a devilish grin, his strums taking on increased enthusiasm.

"No."

"Already taken?"

"Already taken."

"Damn it. All the good ones are always taken. Hmm." He strums for another long beat. "What about 'Purple Rain'?"

I giggle. "Taken."

"*Shit.*"

"So where are we going on tour?" I ask.

Lucas plays an extended version of his riff. "Easier to tell you where we're *not* going." He grins. "And you know where we'll be staying while on tour?" He winks. "Lots and lots of penthouse suites."

I bite my lip. "Sounds delightful."

"Oh, it will be, I assure you." He hums a melody along with his strumming, clearly working something out in his head. "You and me are gonna have fun together like you wouldn't believe. All over the world."

"And what about when we get back from tour?" I ask, suddenly wary. It's just too good to be true. There's got to be a catch.

"The fun will continue," he says simply.

"But where will I live?"

He sings a little line of gibberish as he strums, like he's got the melody line of his new song, just not the actual lyrics yet. "Well, let's see. When we get back from tour," he says, "you're going to live with me at my place in LA. But we'll make lots and lots of visits to New York or wherever else you want to go to make sure you stay nice and happy and never get sick of me."

Elation floods me.

"How's that sound?" he asks. "If that doesn't sound good to you, speak up and we'll make it work. I'm not going to fuck this up."

"It sounds perfect."

Lucas strums and hums for another long moment, his wheels obviously turning. "And then at some point we'll go on tour again. And then we'll come back again for a while. Sprinkle in some awesome vacations, just because we can. Where'd Hand Job take you on vacation? I saw a photo of that fucker on a tropical beach somewhere and you were in the background in a bikini, trying to be invisible, and I knew right then and there you were rocking his world."

"You saw that?"

"I've been stalking you. Where was it?"

"I don't know. It could have been Jamaica. Maybe the Bahamas. Possibly the French Riviera. He took me a few places."

"Motherfucker," Lucas says. "Bastard. Fuck!" He plays his riff again. "Well, wherever that bastard took you, I'm going to take you to way better places. Places that are a thousand times better, I swear to God."

I laugh. "I don't care where we go. I just want to be with you. That's all I've ever wanted."

"Well, you're going to get what you want, and then some." He plays an extended version of his guitar riff again, his eyes boring holes into my flesh as he does. "Okay, Ass-kicker. Don't move a muscle. Looking at you is making this song crash into me like a ton of bricks." He plays an even more elaborate riff followed by a bunch of strumming and humming. "Okay, I've got it now. It's fully formed— just waiting for me to transcribe it." He beams a huge, earnest smile at me that melts my heart. "God, I missed you, Abby."

"I physically ached for you," I say.

"I'm sorry," he says. "I didn't mean to mess with your head. I just had some shit to work out."

I press my lips together, suddenly overwhelmed with emotion. I swallow the lump in my throat. "There's nothing to apologize for. So, do you have a title for your latest masterpiece yet?"

"I sure do. A great title. 'Abby.'"

I burst out laughing. "Taken."

He strums for a long moment again, a wicked smile on his

luscious lips. "'Thriller'?"

"Perfect. I'm absolutely positive that one's never been used before."

He winks and begins playing his extended riff again, this time alternating between strumming and picking his strings, filling the room with the kinds of sounds only Lucas Ford can make. "Okay, baby, seriously now, I've got the perfect song title. Something no other bastard has used in the history of time. It's completely original."

"Is it 'Stairway to Heaven'?" I ask.

He chuckles. "Nope. It's way better than that."

"'Stayin' Alive'?"

He chuckles. "Nope."

"Okay, I give up," I say. "What's the 'completely original' title of your new song, Lucas Ford?"

"'I. Love. You.'"

My heart stops.

Lucas abruptly stops strumming his guitar and puts his hands over the strings. "I love you, Abby. I truly do. I love you and I'm positive I'm not going to want anyone else, ever."

I take a deep, steadying breath. "I love you, too." I crawl to his end of the couch, put my palms on his cheeks, and kiss his delectable lips. "And, my love, there's no doubt in my mind I always will."

MORE MISADVENTURES

VISIT MISADVENTURES.COM
FOR MORE INFORMATION!

MORE MISADVENTURES

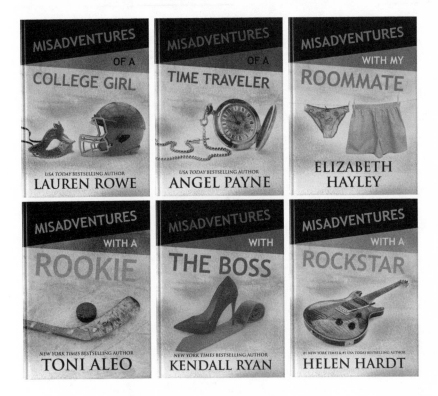

ALSO AVAILABLE FROM
WATERHOUSE PRESS

Keep reading for an excerpt!

CHAPTER ONE

CLARE

My heart pounded so loudly I could hear it. It reverberated through my body, creating an unexpected pulse between my thighs.

We won. *We won!*

I screamed, jumping up and down on the sideline, too overwhelmed with our victory—*Eric's* victory. Eric Hayward was the only player I ever noticed on the football field. Ironically, I don't think he had seen me once in the nearly four years we'd attended high school together. Until his soft brown eyes met mine from across the field. The chaos of the stadium fell to a mere murmur in my mind. Impossibly, my heart raced faster. He shot me a broad, sweet grin that was designed by God to melt teenage girls' panties. My lips parted and curved into a smile.

Then Travis, by far the tallest and best-built player on the field, crashed into Eric with a manly hug. They laughed and hollered with the others, and just that quickly...our connection was broken. A tiny bit of my heart fell, but another part celebrated our brief moment, however fleeting.

I gathered up some of the football equipment from the sideline and carried it into the school. A few minutes later, the team barreled through the doors. I turned, unable to resist the chance to visually appreciate the view of a bunch of hot, sweaty football players.

Eric trailed behind the others. Without his helmet, his sandy brown hair was darkened with sweat and messy from his exertions on the field. Even so, with his flushed cheeks and proud smile, he was irresistible. I couldn't take my eyes off him, and as the rest of the team poured into the locker room, he lingered, until we stood only inches away from each other.

Silence hung in the air between us, but somehow I managed to find my voice. "Congratulations, Eric. You were amazing out there."

Before I knew it, he brought his hand to my face. My heart beat wildly in my chest. First, a look, and now, his touch. Warm and firm. Possessive. Something deep in my core clenched, as I remembered many nights when I would have given anything to have him look at me the way he was looking at me right now.

He bent slightly, and instinctively I reached up toward him, lifting myself on my toes to bring us closer. Presumptuous, maybe, but I wanted that closeness with him, even if he rejected me. But he didn't. Instead, he brought his lips to mine, and his earthy musk filled my lungs. He was tentative only a moment before sliding his palm behind my neck, holding us together. As if I'd had any plans to resist his touch. He probed my mouth with his tongue, and I moaned, because he tasted like lust and confidence...and all the things I imagined someone as untouchable as Eric Hayward would.

I clenched my fists, holding myself back from climbing the beautiful body in front of me. Ten seconds, a minute. I had no idea how long Eric kissed me, but when we parted, I couldn't breathe.

Then I couldn't stop breathing. I might have been hyperventilating, or hallucinating. But damn, I wanted his lips on me again. I wanted his hands. I wanted more of the tease of his tongue on mine and everywhere else. I'd spent so many nights lying in bed, dreaming of the way he'd fuck me—if by some miracle he'd ever notice me in the first place. Heaven help me, I ached for that now more than ever.

His eyes were still bright, energy radiating off him from the win, but his smile had faded. His breath was as ragged as my own. Probably from the adrenaline of winning. It couldn't be from this... from...*me?*

"Damn," he whispered, his gaze trailing over me from head to toe, lighting each part of me on fire. I pressed my hot palms against the cool cinder block wall behind me. Hormones lit up under my skin, causing a fierce ache at the core of me that had never known the touch of a man.

ACKNOWLEDGEMENTS

This book, along with all my others, is dedicated to my wonderful and loyal readers. Thank you for always sticking with me. Thank you also to the talented and kind Meredith Wild and the fabulous team at Waterhouse Press for welcoming me into your publishing family. It's been a true pleasure. And, last but not least, thank you to my dear friend, Stacy Carlson, for the hilarious name of Abby's blog and for always being such a great sounding board for me as I write these stories of mine. You are my own personal Dr. Carlson, Ms. Carlson!

ABOUT LAUREN ROWE

USA Today and internationally bestselling author Lauren Rowe lives in San Diego, California, where, in addition to writing books, she performs with her dance/party band at events all over Southern California, writes songs, takes embarrassing snapshots of her ever-patient Boston terrier, Buster, spends time with her wonderful family, and narrates audiobooks. Much to Lauren's thrill, her books have been translated all over the world in multiple languages and hit multiple domestic and international bestseller lists. With enticing characters, enthralling situations and a general love of romantic fiction, Lauren has created a world of her own, full of wit and sensual desire.

VISIT HER AT LAURENROWEBOOKS.COM!